The Doomed Colony

A Novel

C.E. Bradley

The Doomed Colony

Copyright © 2021 by C.E. Bradley

ISBN: 9798727275160

Part I

To Live and Die on Mars

CHAPTER 1

Sitting in his favorite chair after completing a grueling work-shift at the power plant, Fly waited for his friends. Fly loved Maria's Cantina. One of several establishments, situated in *Café Alley*, Maria's Cantina served authentic Brazilian cuisine. The cantina boasted both indoor and outdoor seating. Both café-style tables and a polish chrome bar provided seating for approximately sixty customers inside the cantina; similarly, generous, roped-off tables provided seating for at least seventy people on the outside. Outside, is where Fly waited for both of his friends—one who worked at the hydroponics plant and the other, who worked with him, at the power plant. Fly sat just behind the ropes that separated the cantina from the thoroughfare. He liked this location because it gave him a chance to watch people. He was usually the first one out of the power plant just so he could secure his favorite table and get people-watching in before his friends arrived.

"What can I get for you sweetie?" Angela asked as she approached his table.

Looking into Angela's brown eyes, Fly flashed her a teasing smile, and replied, "how about a beer along with your company."

Alluringly tilting her head to one side, Angela responded, "a beer you got. But my company belongs to someone else."

Fly watched as Angela walked away after taking his order. He drooled over her fiery eyes and shapely body. "She could do better," he mumbled to himself.

As the work-shifts at the stockyard, hydroponics plant, and power plant changed; people, once again, populated the thoroughfare. The workers' ages ranged from sixteen to twenty-eight years old. Their supervisors' ages ranged from twenty-nine to forty-nine years old. Therefore, the general population that occupied the workers' living spaces were from sixteen to forty-nine years old. Neither children nor anyone over sixty-years of age lived in the workers quarters.

Before Angela returned with Fly's beer, he was joined by his friends: Otto and Alicia.

Almost six-feet tall, with a muscular build and curly blond hair, Otto sat next to Fly. "I am definitely going to try out this time," Otto said with an engaging grin.

Although best friends, the two young men could have not looked more different. Fly's slender frame, dark-brown skin, and tightly curled hair contrasted evenly to Otto's taller, thicker body-frame, blond hair, and porcelain skin. In the old world, they could have been a Nigerian marathoner and a German soccer player.

Alicia winked at Otto, and said, "I think your songs are really good, but" she paused while eyeing Fly, "you have very stiff competition."

Whenever Otto looked at Alicia, he could not help but smile. He loved the dark-brown eyes that sat above those full, inviting lips.

"Here you go sweetie," Angela said as she placed Fly's beer in front of him. Then looking at Alicia and Otto, she asked, "what can I get you two?"

"I'll also have a beer," Alicia answered.

"Make that two," Otto chimed in.

Angela scanned the outside seating, smiled, and said, "looks like we are filling up with customers. I'll be back in a few minutes with your drinks and get your food orders."

Upon Angela's departure, Fly said, "I am going to try out also. I have been working on a few songs that just might put me in the top-ten of talent." Then turning his attention to Alicia, he asked, "are you trying out for the talent show?"

Knowing that she had neither the talent nor the inclination to perform, Alicia answered, "that's not for me. But I will support you two. I will be in the front row cheering you on."

The two young men both inwardly smiled knowing that they had the support of a young woman who they equally sought after. Alicia, on the other hand, could not think beyond the disturbing dreams she had been having for the last two weeks. Those shadowy dreams clouded most of her thoughts.

CHAPTER 2

After another night of disturbing dreams, Alicia stood in front the aquaponics plant's teaching display. Alicia had two equally important jobs at the aquaponics plant. Her first job was to provide laborious upkeep of the plant and animal life; and her second job was to educate the public about the plant's operations. In the past, she briefed heads of state, students, and sometimes families. Today, she found herself standing in front of a group of privileged teenagers.

"Aquaponics," she began, "is a subset of hydroculture. Hydroculture is a method of growing plants without soil. Instead of soil we use a mineral-nutrient solution. At the aquaponics plant we grow enough plants for our entire Martian colony...", then noticing a rugged-looking teen with his hand up, she asked, "do you have a question?"

"*Da,* I mean Yes, I do," the young man answered with an engaging smile. "You said that the plants are grown without soil. Is that correct?"

Noticing his thick, Russian accent, Alicia assumed this young man the son of one of the highest-level oligarchs. "That is correct," she replied.

"If there is no soil," he continued, "then where do the nutrients come from?"

"That is a very good question," she complimented. "Aquaponics is a combination of aquaculture—where seafood is farmed; and horticulture—where plants are farmed." She then pointed to the aquaponics display which revealed a simplistic version of the complicated process. The display consisted of two tanks with one on top of the other. The tank on the top displayed small, dainty plants with their roots immersed in water while the tank at bottom presented fish swimming around. On both sides of the tanks, were two, large tubes that connected them.

"In this display, you will notice plants in the top tank and fish in the bottom one. Well, to answer your question, the nutrients used in the hydroponic system come from the fish excrement. And, in turn, after the plants uptake these nutrients they cleanse the water which is, subsequently, returned to the fish."

"You mean," said a pretty, perky blond girl in the front of the crowd, "that our food has poop in it?"

Getting this same question every time, Alicia nodded.

"*Poop*, as you so nicely put it, is just a type of fertilizer," Alicia answered. "We have always applied fertilizers for growing food. Back on Earth, farmers used all types of excrement to grow plants—horse manure was a common one."

"That sucks," the girl said with a scour. "I am going to tell my Daddy and he will make you use something else."

"What an ingenious way to grow our food," the rough-looking, young man chimed in. "Are there other benefits to this system?"

Glad to get off the excrement subject, Alicia said with a nod, "yes, we also get fresh oxygen from this system."

"How fascinating," the young man said as some of the group began to break up and walk away. "Is it possible I can get your contact information so that I can learn more?"

Although Alicia did not find this privileged teen as disgusting as most of them, she cringed at continuing any dialogue with him.

She shook her head, and said, "I am sorry, but I really don't have the time. I do have to work for a living."

With that, she turned and walked away.

After a very productive, but tiring day of work, Alicia decided not to gather with Fly and Otto at their usual hangout. Instead, she went home. Her mother greeted her at the two-bedroom apartment they shared. Her mother, Pythia, seated at the kitchen table pointed at the chair across from her, and said, "sit, and tell me about your dreams."

Although drained from her workday, Alicia always brightened up in her mother's presence—especially when she wanted to know about her dreams. When she sat across from her mother, it seemed as if an entire weight was lifted.

After Alicia was seated, Pythia went to the kitchen and reappeared with a large bowl of soup, and two smaller bowls. "Help yourself sweetie," she said then went back to the kitchen.

Alicia ladled herself a bowl of seafood soup.

Upon returning with a garden-green salad and a piping-hot loaf of bread, Pythia placed them on the table. Then seeing that the table was prepared to her satisfaction, Pythia, once again, sat across from Alicia and ladled herself a helping of the seafood soup.

Alicia tasted the soup, and said with a huge sigh, "this is so delicious momma. Now, about my dream—I don't know where to begin."

"At the beginning, dear," Pythia said with an encouraging smile that was as warm as the soup.

"Okay momma. At first, I was standing on a lush, green mountain that was located on Earth. All around me were thriving trees. Earth was at peace. Unlike the Earth we left, it was a planet without rumors of wars. And I, along with many other people, were planting more trees to make the mountain flourish." Alicia paused, added butter to her bread, took another sip of the soup, then continued. "The sun so warmed my skin and the birds loudly chirped. After planting three more trees, I sat down on the warm earth to take a drink of water from my canteen. While drinking the water, I noticed a segmented worm that was approximately three inches long. I think it was an earthworm. It crawled up on my leg. Oddly enough, I was not squeamish about the contact; I just gently picked it up and held it at eye level. And in some strange way, the contact with the squirmy, little creature soothed me."

Remembering the worm brought a smile to her face. But, just as quickly as the smile appeared, her eyes grew tearful and she began to tremble.

"The earth, beneath us, began to shake," Alicia continued. As the earth shook, the little worm turned into Grandfather and stood beside me. But no matter how comforting Grandfather was, I was afraid of what I saw next."

Noticing Alicia's frightened look, Pythia said, "go on sweetie, you can tell me."

Alicia hesitated to continue while pushing salad greens around in her bowl.

Reaching across the table, Pythia gently touched Alicia's hand and nodded encouragingly.

Knowing that she had no reason to fear this creature, Alicia boldly continued. "There appeared creature, who looked like a skeleton. He danced up the mountain towards us. He wore a necklace with eyeballs dangling from it. In one hand he held a smoking cigarette and with the other hand he began to pull our newly planted trees from the ground. As he approached us the earthquakes became violent."

Clearly shaken, Alicia paused, once again. She pushed her chair away from the table and stood up. Pythia watched as her daughter paced back and forth. After a few moments of silence, Alicia continued.

"After the earth shook, the sky darkened. Next, a cool breeze blew. And, with the breeze came a large crocodile who arrogantly swaggered towards us. And, with the crocodile came a chilling fear. The fear enveloped me. I could not move. I could not breathe. I just stood there. Afraid!"

Seeing that her daughter was clearly shaken, Pythia stood, wrapped an arm around Alicia's trembling shoulders, and guided her to the living room where she gently lowered her to the sofa. Pythia then retrieved Alicia's water from the table, placed it in her hands, and said, "drink this sweetie. I want you to relax for a while. I have enough information from your dream to begin an interpretation."

CHAPTER 3

Like Alicia, Otto and Fly were spokespeople for their power plant. Also, like Alicia, they found themselves facing a group of privileged teens who lived in the upper-society dome. However, unlike Alicia, both Otto and Fly enjoyed mingling with the upper-class. The more people they knew, the better their chances of winning the talent competition.

"This power plant provides all the energy we need to survive on Mars. The energy we take for granted until it is gone," said Fly. "For example, without energy generated at the plant, we would not have electricity to cook our food, heat or cool our homes, and wash our clothes."

A seventeen-year-old girl raised her hand, and asked, "where does the energy come from?"

"That is a very good question," Otto replied. "My friend and I work at different parts of the power plant. I mainly work at the part of the plant that converts both solar and wind energy into electricity; and both my buddy, Fly and I, work at the division of the plant that converts geothermal energy into electricity."

"How is geothermal energy obtained?" Asked a rough-looking young man with a Russian accent.

"Geothermal energy is nothing more than the internal heat that is contained in the rocks and fluids beneath Mars' surface. We harvest this heat, in the form of steam from which we generate electricity," Fly explained.

"So, do you need to drill for this energy?"

"Absolutely," Fly acknowledged. "As a matter of fact, we have a few drilling projects in the works to obtain a more stable supply of energy."

"What about the solar and wind energy?" Interrupted the teenage girl.

"Well," started Otto, "we have an array of solar panels as well as an enormous wind farm located outside of the domes. Since this planet gets direct sunlight and has sweeping windstorms, we won't run out of energy for quite some time."

Again, the rough-looking young man switched the conversation back to geothermal energy. "If we have all of the energy we need from the solar panels and wind turbines, why do we need to drill for more geothermal energy?"

"That is an excellent question," Fly answered with a smile. "By the way, what is your name?"

"Gregory," the young man answered.

"Well Gregory," Fly began, "although our colony presently live within three bio-domes, we are planning for the future. Presently, one dome houses everything we need to sustain us: the aquaponics plant, the energy plants, and the animal farms; the second dome houses most of the population—mainly the working class; and the third dome houses the entertainment venues along with the families of the decision makers. And, although we have enough energy for now, the decision makers want us to expand our colony."

"Expand?" Gregory asked.

"Yes, they are hoping to create more spaces for living—at least that is what I am told."

"So, you need to find more sources of energy. The more spaces we occupy, the more energy we need," concluded Otto.

Fly nodded in agreement.

After a moment of silence, Gregory asked, "may I speak with you about this later? I have so many questions."

Glad to be of assistance to one of the privileged few, Fly grinned and nodded.

CHAPTER 4

Although Fly lived in the Martian colony for three years, he had never been to the bio-dome occupied by the upper-class. When only fifteen years of age, he was hurried out of bed in the middle of the night by his mother and father. They informed him that they were going on a long journey. And even though he argued with them about leaving his friends and his neighborhood, he had no say-so in the matter. After they crowded him in the back seat of their sports-utility-vehicle with as much luggage as they could take, his parents sped away from their San Diego, California home. And they never looked back.

Both of Fly's parents were scientists: his mother a geophysicist and his father an astrophysicist. For a year before they left Earth, he knew that things were not quite right. For one thing, both his parents were vague about their workdays. Years before, all they talked about were their individual scientific worlds. Then in the last year before they left their San Diego home, they both became secretive; both distancing themselves from family and friends. Although Fly thought that his parents' behavior was odd, he never guessed that they were both part of a master plan to create the first Martian colony. How could he have known since manned spaceflight outside of Earth's orbit was simply an idea on the drawing board.

And here he was on Mars walking from one bio-dome to another. As he walked through the long hallway that connected Bio-2 to Bio-1, he looked up at the pink, Martian sky. The domes' outer covering was transparent and made of a material that sustained the impact of an average meteor strike. Also hermetically sealed, the domes' covering prevented the passage of gasses—very airtight. So, as Fly walked down the long hallway he lazily looked up at the pink sky in excited anticipation.

He was excited to be invited to Bio-1. None of his friends had ever been there. Besides, to enter Bio-1 one needed to be a resident, invited by a resident, be a day worker at one of the many retail outlets or restaurants, or win the talent competition. He only saw Bio-1's inhabitants when they came around for a tour of the power plant. Since Fly's day-to-day life consisted of working at the geothermal plant's drill site, hanging with his friends at Maria's Cantina, and composing lyrics to his previously composed beats; he hardly had time to consider what life in Bio-1 was like.

14

So, when Gregory—one of the privileged teens who toured the power plant—invited Fly to meet him at Bio-1 for an afternoon drink where they could discuss more about geothermal energy, Fly faked an illness to get off work early and headed straight for Bio-1.

Although crime was nonexistent in the Martian colony, security at Bio-1's entrance was strict. Before Fly came to within a yard of the door, he was met by two, security guards. Wearing all black and carrying rifles, these guards were intimidating.

"Citizen, show identification," said the taller guard.

Nervously, Fly reached into his pants pocket and pulled out the standard picture identification that all colonists carried. Then, trying not to be overwhelmed by his nerves while he handed the guard his identification card, he held his head high and stared straight in the security guard's eyes.

Staring back at Fly with a scowl, the guard snatched his identification card and scrutinized it. During this time, the other guard stepped forward, nodded, and said, "state your purpose citizen. Why are you here?"

Before Fly answered, Gregory appeared at Bio-1's entrance, and said, "he is here to see me. I invited him here."

When the guards saw who belonged to the voice, they immediately stiffened.

"Oh, Master Gregory!" Said the guard who was examining Fly's identification card. The guard hastily returned Fly's card with a slight bow.

15

"Don't mind them," Gregory said to Fly. "They are just doing their jobs." Gregory then nodded his head towards the entrance, and said, "I have a couple of beers waiting for us." Upon entering Bio-1, Fly immediately noticed the difference between Bio-1 and Bio-2. Although the domes were identical from the outside, inside was another matter. Fly observed that not only was the sky brighter, but the air was cleaner. As Gregory led him to the central square, Fly took a deep breath of the fresher air and savored the differences in ambience. For one thing, instead of crowded rows of bars and restaurants, there were spacious areas which included parks with rows of trees and plants. Instead of streets crowded with workers either going to work or going home from work, there were luxury, clothing shops with shoppers leisurely walking while carrying their purchases. And, instead of cantinas there were outdoor eateries.

"Here we are," Gregory said when he stopped at a table at the café. "I ordered you a beer. I hope you don't mind."

Fly smiled, sat down opposite Gregory, and said, "I don't mind at all."

After taking a sip of the refreshing beer, Gregory stared at Fly from across the table. Looking at a man his same age, Gregory observed that although Fly's face held the wonderment of youth, it also held a slight sadness.

"So, tell me about your work at the geothermal plant," Gregory requested.

Fly sipped his beer, and said, "I am a member of the drill crew. Mostly, I make sure that when we are drilling, the

16

pressure gauges are within tolerance levels." He took another sip of the brew, shrugged his shoulders, and continued, "I am just an apprentice. And, one day—when I am deemed ready by my supervisor—I can move up in status at the plant."

Gregory nodded, and asked, "isn't subsurface drilling a danger to this planet? Back on Earth, there were many earthquakes associated with *fracking*. This fracking process, where liquid is injected at high pressures into subterranean rocks, boreholes, etc., forces open existing fissures to extract both oil and gas. That pressure-forcing is thought to cause earthquakes."

Although Fly wanted to impress Gregory, he knew nothing about the science that went into drilling for energy. All he knew was his part as a drill-team member. "Well, my friend," Fly replied, "I can't help you there. But my mother is a geophysicist—and a member of the power-plant's science board—she may have answers for you."

With heightened attention, Gregory leaned across the table, and asked, "is there any way that I could meet your mother?"

Fly nodded, and said, "of course. Are you free for dinner tomorrow night?"

Eager to talk to Fly's mother, but out of years of etiquette, Gregory sat back in his seat, and replied, "I don't want to impose."

Fly threw his head back with a hearty laugh, and said, "impose? Not on your life! Besides me, there are two things that my mother love. Those are hosting parties and her

17

profession. So no, you will not impose. You will brighten her day."

Gregory eagerly nodded, and said, "in that case, I accept. Dinner tomorrow night. Now, can I do anything for you?"

Enthusiastically nodding, Fly replied, "yes, you can show me around Bio-1. Mostly, the theater where the talent competition is held. My buddy and I are going to compete this year."

Gregory graciously bowed his head as he said, "I'm at your service."

CHAPTER 5

After a challenging, yet, curious day of work at the
animal husbandry farm, Pythia sat on her living-room sofa,
kicked off her shoes, enjoyed a glass of wine, and waited for
her daughter to arrive home from the aquaponics plant. As a
top-notch veterinarian, Pythia ensured a viable livestock for the
Martian colony. It was her responsibility to keep the animals
disease-free, able to breed, and sustainable.

Along with Pythia, thirty others managed the animals.
During the day, one of the herdsmen sought her out concerning
a cow. The hefty bovine seemed exceptionally sluggish and
disorientated. Pythia told the herdsman to immediately isolate
the animal and send its blood, urine, and stool samples to the
laboratory for analysis. Although she suspected nothing more
than an upset stomach or pregnancy, she never ruled anything
out when it came to the safety of their food supply.

After her husband, along with five other scientists, died a year ago in an unexplained accident, Pythia's time was consumed between work and Alicia. In the wake of her husband's death, she fell into a deep depression. She abused alcohol and refused to get out of bed. If it were not for Alicia's gentle encouragement, she would have never recovered from the heartbreaking loss. And although she missed her husband every day, the profound love she felt for her daughter reawakened her to life.

"Come have a seat," Pythia said as Alicia entered their apartment.

Alicia hung her sweater and backpack on hooks near door. She then fetched a wine glass from the kitchen's cabinet, poured herself a portion from the opened wine bottle, and sat next to Pythia.

Alicia planted a kiss on her mother's cheek, took a sip of wine, and looked at her mother excitedly.

Smiling at her daughter, Pythia nodded her head, and said, "I have an interpretation of your dream."

Alicia's eyes widened in silent anticipation. Even though her mother was an expert veterinarian by profession, her spiritual beliefs were rooted in a long line of Mayan shamans.

"Well, my dear, your dream has both good and bad news for us all."

Alicia was silent.

"The good news is that we have a protector. The worm you spoke of who turned into my father was there to guide us

20

through difficult times that we must face. His name is *Mam*. He is a powerful Mayan god."

Alicia took another sip of her wine, and asked with a shaky voice, "and, the dancing skeleton with the eyeball necklace?"

"He is *Cizin*. *Cizin*, or otherwise known as *Xibalba*, is the Mayan earthquake god and god of death; he is the ruler of the subterranean land of the dead."

Alicia gasped, then asked, "and, the crocodile?"

"He is *Zipacna*," Pythia answered. "He is a very violent and arrogant demon. He is also associated with earthquakes."

Alicia took a deep breath, and asked, "what does it all mean momma?"

"As a first interpretation," Pythia began, "the act of planting trees—in your dream—represents the roots we are putting down in this Martian colony. The crocodile or, *Zipacna*, represents a violent event that might befall us— possibly a Mars-quake. The dancing skeleton, or *Cizin*, represents our fate following the violent event—possibly death and destruction. However, the worm, or *Mam*, represents some sort of salvation—possibly an escape from the event."

Alicia thought about this for a few moments, then asked, "momma, are you saying that this colony is doomed?"

Pythia nodded in agreement.

"When will it happen?"

Pythia thought a while, then replied, "it may happen tomorrow. It may happen in fifty years. It may happen in three-thousand years."

21

Considering that there was some urgency associated with her dream, Alicia, unquestionably, knew that they had little time.

"How will we know when the event is near?"

Noticing her daughter's anxiety-laden eyes, Pythia responded, "relax darling. There is nothing we can do until additional warnings appear. And the only way we will recognize the warnings is if we are relaxed." With those words she gave her daughter a reassuring, comforting smile.

CHAPTER 6

Gregory, son of the most powerful aristocrat on Mars—
Boris Andreevich—hailed from a long line of Russian royals.
Before the Bolshevik Revolution, the Andreevichs were tied to
Czars either through bloodlines or businesses. All through
Russia's socialist period, the family secretly managed to
maintain economic holdings while spreading their financial
influences worldwide. After the *Iron Curtain* fell, the family
resurfaced as an unquestionable power. They not only made
money on Russia's black-market, but they also used their
money to buy political favors from international countries.

The Andreevichs—along with five other, old-money
billionaires from around the world—set in motion plans to
control the twenty-first century. Through their money and
power, they placed puppets at the heads of many powerful

countries. Whether these puppets were presidents or prime ministers, they were secretly, yet masterfully, controlled by the six architects of the twenty-first century. These six architects, the *New Guard*, not only manipulated the world's politics but also controlled the world's financial markets.

However, when the New Guard realized that the useful idiots which they placed at the heads of countries were setting the Earth on a ruinous path, they covertly planned to colonize the red planet: Mars.

During the time that his father was manipulating human society, Gregory was still an innocent child. And even when taken to the Martian colony he had no knowledge that his father—along with five of the richest men on Earth—was responsible for the destruction of their home planet. It was not until his older brother, Yuri, died that Gregory's eyes were opened. He found Yuri's diary. The diary detailed how the New Guard was responsible for the destruction of Earth; and, if left unchecked, they would be responsible for the same destruction of Mars. Moreover, the diary documented Yuri's secret meetings with the scientists of Bio-2. The last entry in Yuri's diary was dated the day before he and several scientists were found dead outside Bio-3 where their bodies were exposed to Mars' deadly atmosphere.

Determined to understand his older brother's diary and to possibly ward off any future destruction of the planet he now calls home, Gregory jumped at the chance to meet with Fly's mother. So, with long-stemmed roses in hand, he stood in front of Fly's home. Enthusiastically, he rang the doorbell. Within seconds, Fly greeted Gregory with a warm handshake and ushered him inside.

Before the two, young men made conversation, a petite woman with a frank smile appeared at Fly's side. Sporting the same dark-brown skin and tightly curled hair as Fly, Gregory saw that she was, unmistakably, Fly's mother.

With a bow of his head, Gregory extended the roses to the petite woman, and said, "these are for you, Doctor Greyson."

"Oh, how lovely," Doctor Greyson said as she took the roses.

Gregory breathed in the ubiquitously wonderful aroma, then genuinely said, "something smells delicious."

"Mama's cooking," Fly said, "is the best you will ever have."

Before Doctor Greyson had a chance to continue the conversation, once again, the doorbell rang. With a kind smile, Doctor Greyson handed the roses to Fly then said to Gregory, "please call me Cheryl. And I hope you do not mind, but I also invited others to join us."

"Come on," Fly nodded his head towards the kitchen, "I need to put these into a vase. My mom always enjoys parties."

As Gregory followed Fly towards the kitchen, the two-bedroom apartment began to fill with other guests.

Leaning against the kitchen's counter while Fly sliced off an inch of the roses' bottom stems, Gregory said, "your mother seems very nice."

25

Fly opened one of the kitchen's cabinets, retrieved a flower vase from the top shelf, and said, "not only is she smart and can cook, but she is also the kindest person I've ever known."

Gregory watched as Fly filled the vase with water, retrieved an aspirin from another cabinet, and plopped it into the vase. "Why did you put an aspirin in the water?" He asked.

"Oh, mama says that an aspirin opens up the stem's cell-membrane which allows the flowers to absorb water easily," he answered then carefully placed the flowers into the vase.

Before Gregory asked another question, one of the guests found her way into the kitchen.

"Alicia, I would like you to meet Gregory," Fly said with the vase of roses in hand. "Would you mind keeping him company while I put these flowers on the table in the dining room?"

Without waiting for a reply, Fly breezed by Alicia and headed for the dining room.

Alicia sized up Gregory, and asked, "don't I know you? You look familiar."

Pleased to be in Alicia's company, Gregory nodded, and replied, "I was a visitor to the aquaponics plant. With the amount of people who you lecture to, I am amazed that you recognize me."

Alicia nodded. "The man with many questions," she affirmed.

26

Gregory blushed. As his body temperature rose, he knew that his face reddened. He hated that. Being in the presence of a smart and beautiful girl stunned him silent.

Alicia noticed Gregory's discomfort. She was pleasingly aware of her physical appearance and the effect it had on boys. Amusingly, she watched as sweat formed on Gregory's forehead. Then mercifully, she asked, "did you have any more questions for me about the aquaponics process?"

As sweat rolled down his forehead towards his eyes, he answered, "yes. What are your duties at the plant? How many hours do you work there?"

"I ensure that the sea creatures are healthy. I evaluate their environment daily, see that they are reproducing regularly, and that their population is sustainable—making sure that we do not over-harvest them. And to answer your second question, like everyone in Bio-2, I work eight-hours a day for five days a week."

Gregory considered this worker society; a society that he took for granted. All his life, he was catered to. He always had enough food, cloths, and shelter. He never wondered how many people worked most of their lives to provide these necessities. While his days were consumed with some schoolwork, friends, and sporting activities; Alicia, and others like her, were working to make life livable for everyone. After listening to Alicia, he realized that social structure had more meaning. He wanted to ask more questions about her living conditions, about her family—did she have a family? However, before he opened his mouth to speak, a burly teenager—about the same age as him—entered the kitchen. The teen positioned himself next to Alicia.

"Gregory, this is my friend, Otto," Alicia introduced.

The two young men of equal stature hesitantly shook hands.

Broodingly, Otto glared at Gregory.

Feeling the heightened testosterone level between the two young men, Alicia said, "excuse me. I have to see if Cheryl needs help with anything."

Fly passed by Alicia on his way into the kitchen.

Upon entering the kitchen, Fly instantly became aware of hostile stares Otto and Gregory were exchanging, and said, "I see you two are acquainted." Then looking at Otto's aggressive posture, Fly said, "hey man, how about we perform one of our songs for the crowd out there?"

Although he heard Fly's request, Otto narrowed his eyes as if to shoot laser beams at Gregory.

Annoyed by Otto's inattentiveness, Fly yanked his friend's sleeve, and said, "come on. Help me set up my instruments."

Before Fly had a chance to invite Gregory along, he heard his mom's voice calling everyone to dinner.

The dining-room's table was set up buffet-style with food at one end and dinnerware at the other. Although Cheryl cooked a large pot of Gumbo—a dish she ate every Sunday as a native from New Orleans—other guests such as Otto's father and Alicia's mother brought their favorite dishes. Following Fly's lead, people grabbed a plate and filled it up with one

28

delicacy after another then found a place to sit in the already crowded living room.

When seeing Gregory sitting alone on a stool by the mantle, Cheryl pulled a stool close to his, sat down, and said, "I hope you get to meet others at this gathering. You might be surprised the things you will learn."

After consuming a heaping spoonful of the gumbo, Gregory exclaimed, "this is fabulous! I don't think I've tasted anything like it in my life."

Cheryl bowed her head, and said, "thank you. It was my mother's recipe."

Gregory downed several more gulps of the delicious, seafood dish and filled his mouth with so much food that he could not speak.

"I know that you weren't expecting a party, but I just couldn't help myself," Cheryl said with a chuckle. "Now, Fly tells me that you want to learn more about our geothermal harvesting techniques. Why don't you stop by my office around nine tomorrow morning? I will try to answer your questions."

Anxious to talk, Gregory worked hard to swallow the mouthful of delicious food; he nearly choked. Finally, clearing his mouth, he said, "that would be awesome."

Once Cheryl departed to address other guests, Alicia took her seat.

Although he mainly came to talk to Fly's mother, Gregory happily welcomed Alicia's company.

"So, where on Earth did your family come from?" Alicia asked.

"Although my family lived in Moscow for many years, we originally came from a small town near the Caucasus Mountains called Grozny. What about you? Where did your family live on Earth?"

Alicia smiled warmly. She remembered growing up in El Salvador with its warm climate and rich Mayan history. She then took a taste of the meal that her mother, Pythia, brought to the party: Pupusas. This El Salvadoran staple food—made of corn tortillas, stuffed with cheese, pork rinds, and beans—almost brought sentimental tears to Alicia's eyes.

After swallowing her forkful of home, she answered, "my family lived in El Salvador until we came to Mars."

Before the two had a chance to continue their conversation, both Fly and Otto stood near the door which led out to the patio and began rapping lyrics to the beats of previously composed music. Even though everyone continued to enjoy their food, they attentively listened to the rap which consisted mostly of homesick tales from the planet they left behind.

During the performance, Gregory looked at the faces of everyone at the party and realized that he had lived in the wrong bio-dome.

CHAPTER 7

Just like every workday on Mars, Fly donned his environmental suit and hopped into the utility vehicle. Along with six other vehicles—each occupied with two people—Fly drove his vehicle out of Bio-3's hangar and onto the Martian surface. However, unlike any other day, he carried a passenger. A teenage girl from Bio-1, who had previously toured the geothermal plant, accompanied him. Although Fly preferred to work alone, he could not turn down a request from a possible fan from Bio-1.

"First, thank you so much for allowing me to accompany you during your workday. And second, can you explain exactly what your job entails?" Asked Heather.

"If you remember from your tour, we are drilling for a deeper source of geothermal energy. And this vehicle contains the instrument package needed for drilling."

31

Tilting her head to one side, Heather shot Fly an inquisitive look, and asked, "instruments?"

"Yes, these instruments measure: the heat and pressure of the drill bit, everyone's vital signs, and the atmosphere around the drill site; ensuring that the crew can avoid any toxic gases that might escape from the ground."

As they drove along Mars' Tharsis Bulge under the extremely bright, pink sky, Heather—not paying attention to Fly's explanation of the vehicle's instrument package—loudly gasped at the sight of the largest volcano in the solar system: Olympus Mons.

Fly, who never tired of seeing the massive volcano, smiled. Towering 16 miles above the Martian surface, Olympus Mons eclipsed three Mount Everests stacked on top of one another.

"That is an amazing vision," Fly said.

"I've seen it on our tele-teaching screens in the classroom. But that does it no justice," Heather insisted.

"Well, as a tidbit of knowledge," Fly began, "the reason we are settled on the Tharsis Bulge is because of its dormant volcanic activity. Our scientists realized that even though the volcanos are dormant, that there must still be an abundance of heat just below the surface for us to use as energy."

Heather fell silent as she marveled at the gigantic volcano.

"Okay," said Fly, "we are here at the site. Although we will be fifty feet from the actual drilling, you can still see the activity from here."

Heather smiled. She could hardly contain her excitement. "Can we get out of the vehicle?" She asked.

Fly shrugged his shoulders and replied, "of course. The monitoring panel is located on the outside of the vehicle. Now a few things you need to know. First, and foremost, make sure that your environmental suit is properly sealed. And second, when we get out of the vehicle we will be walking in Mars' gravity. It is lighter than the gravity we experience in the bio-domes so you will have to slow your movements."

Heather's smile turned to a teeth-baring grin. She watched as Fly disembarked and did her best to mimic his movements.

Humorously, Fly watched as Heather disembarked. Remembering the first time he walked on Mars' surface in an environmental suit and how difficult it was for him to maintain a normal gait, he sympathized.

Fly removed the vehicle's back covering and revealed a large computer screen that measured the entire dimensions of the back of the vehicle.

"This screen is divided into quadrants—four different views of the drill-site's activities," Fly said to Heather as he pointed at the screen. "The upper right quadrant contains pressure and temperature gages."

Looking at the upper right screen Heather saw computer-generated instruments that looked like thermometers and numbers flashing next to them.

"The upper left quadrant is a live feed from the drill site," Fly said.

Heather found this screen more interesting since she saw workers who used equipment to drill into the Martian surface. She then pointed to the lower left screen, and asked, "what is this?"

"Another live feed," Fly replied. "This feed is from a camera connected near the end of the drill bit. So, what you are seeing here is the actual soil that we are drilling through." Fly switched his attention to the last screen which contained figures of twelve environmental suits. Each figure had a name above it and their vital signs below it such as: oxygen level, blood pressure, heart rate, and body temperature. "These twelve figures represent us and our drilling crew. And the numbers below them represent our health shown by different vital signs. It is equally important that we keep an eye on both the drilling statistics such as the temperature and pressure gauges as it is important to keep an eye on our vital signs."

"How exciting," Heather said. For the first time in a long time, she felt alive.

CHAPTER 8

Gregory stood in front of Cheryl's desk viewing an electronic, visual monitor that span the upper half of the wall located behind her desk. Cheryl stood next to the viewscreen while pointing to a diagram. The diagram showed the basic layout of the Martian colony.

Cheryl pointed to three hemispheres connected by enclosed walkways, and said, "so this is us. Bios-1, 2, and 3."

Knowing this configuration for the last three years, Gregory sighed and remained silent.

With a flick of her hand the area of the viewscreen changed. Now, the bio-domes were merely a small part of the image. As the bio-domes' sizes shrunk in comparison to the larger countryside, Mars' Tharsis Bulge—along with its four massive volcanos—came into view. Three volcanos: Arsia Mons, Pavonis Mons, and Ascraeus Mons, were aligned a distance from the most massive volcano in the solar system: Olympus Mons. As a geophysicist, Cheryl never tired of such geologic marvels.

"A little history about this region," Cheryl began. "Although Mars boasts about twenty volcanos; the shield volcano, Olympus Mons, stands out. Olympus Mons is often cited as the largest volcano in the solar system. However, by some metrics, other volcanoes are considerably larger. Alba Mons, northeast of Olympus Mons, has roughly nineteen times the surface area, but is only about one-third the height," she said as she pointed to the cone-shaped mounds on the image.

"Moreover, some scientists believe that the Tharsis Bulge is what is known as a super-volcano."

Gregory looked over the image with its large bulge and the four cone-shaped, volcanic mountains that sat on it like breasts resting on a bloated, pig's belly. Visually, it looked harmless, like the Caucasus Mountains which stretched between the Black and Caspian Seas. However, hearing an ominous word associated with the visuals, he asked, "what is a super-volcano?"

Realizing that she was not speaking to a scientist, Cheryl collected her thoughts, and asked, "have you heard of Yellowstone National Park, located in the United States?"

Gregory nodded.

"Well, Yellowstone is a super-volcano. Beneath Yellowstone's surface lies a massive chamber of molten rock, otherwise known as magma. This chamber is constantly filling with toxic gases and magma. In the distant past, when

Yellowstone erupted, it was an event that was a thousand times more powerful than a regular volcanic eruption where at least 240 cubic miles of material was ejected. This eruption possibly lasted for weeks or months."

Gregory silently nodded while Cheryl spoke, signifying his grasp of the subject.

"As I said, some scientists compare the Tharsis Bulge to the Yellowstone super-volcano. Only, as you can see—like most things on Mars—this bulge, and its accompanying volcanos, cover much more area than Yellowstone," Cheryl said.

Gregory nodded.

Cheryl continued, and said, "as I mentioned, this magma chamber feeds the other volcanos on the planet. It is by far the largest volcanic structure in the solar system. Now, Olympus Mons is the youngest of these large volcanoes on Mars, having formed during Mars' Hesperian Period."

"What is Mars' Hesperian Period?" Gregory interrupted. "And how long ago was it?"

"Forgive me," Cheryl apologized. "I got so wrapped up in the science that I forgot I had an audience. So, the Hesperian is a geologic time-period on Mars; it was approximately 3.5 billion years ago. It is characterized by widespread volcanic activity and catastrophic flooding that carved immense outflow channels across the Martian surface. The Hesperian was an intermediate and transitional period of Martian history. During the Hesperian, Mars changed from a

37

wetter, and perhaps, warmer world to the dry, cold, and dusty planet seen today."

Trying to grasp all this information Gregory stood silent.

"Now," Cheryl continued, "because this region was once volcanically active, it stands to reason that there are large magma chambers below the surface. These chambers possibly contain an unlimited energy source."

"I do understand that we have all the energy we need presently and that the city planners want to expand our colony, but won't drilling into this volcanic powder-keg awaken its dormancy?" Gregory finally asked.

Cheryl always liked an inquisitive mind. However, knowing Gregory's father—the most powerful aristocrat on Mars—and remembering how her husband along with five other scientists met their mysterious deaths outside of the bio-domes; Cheryl remained cautious.

"Theoretically," she replied.

Gregory, keenly aware of Cheryl's caution, sat down on a chair facing her desk. Taking the cue, Cheryl sat on the chair behind her desk. The two stared at each other for a few, silent seconds.

Gregory looked around Cheryl's office which barely fit the desk and chairs. Comparing this brilliant scientist's office-space to the same size of his bedroom's closet, Gregory felt ashamed. He was ashamed that he lived in Bio-1 which was the same size as Bio-2 but occupied by a third less people. He was ashamed that he only knew a life of luxury while someone who worked as hard as Cheryl to become so well educated had an office space as small as his bedroom's closet. Gregory put his shame aside knowing that he had to get the answers he sought. And, to get those answers that he desperately wanted depended upon obtaining Cheryl's trust.

As he stared into Cheryl's dark-brown eyes, he said, "I know that your husband, along with other scientists, died last year."

Cheryl silently stared at Gregory.

"And I know that it was no accident."

Cheryl took note of Gregory's thick Russian accent. She observed his aristocratic baring: the straight posture, the fluidic mannerisms, and the deliberate speech. She also noticed the desperate pleas that poured from his eyes. She asked, "what do you mean that it wasn't an accident?"

"I believe that they were forcefully removed from the bio-dome without their environmental suits."

Cheryl felt uncomfortable. She also suspected this to be the case. However, she knew how the secret police worked. Before they departed Earth there were many people that disappeared from their homes with little explanation. Across the globe riots broke out against governments. Because the government leaders' only interest was greed—how they could profit from the people they governed—and not how to protect their people from harm and hunger; discouraged people took to the streets to oust their leaders. During the many street riots against the government, Cheryl kept silent. Not only was she and her husband immersed in their science—preparing for their secret spaceflight to Mars—but they also feared for the safety of their family. Consequently, both Cheryl and her husband were never involved in those riots.

Shifting in her chair, she asked, "so, you believe that they were murdered? Why were they murdered?"

"Because my brother was amongst them. I saw his body when it was brought home. It had all of the signs of exposure to the Martian environment."

Cheryl gasped. She remembered her husband's body when it was brought back into the bio-dome. With his mouth opened and eyes bulged out of his head, he looked like he died horribly gasping for breath. She silently lowered her head.

"And I found his diary. Before he died, my brother, Yuri, met with your husband and other scientists who were concerned about the drilling project."

Noticing the desperation flowing from Gregory's eyes, she said, "obviously, we knew of our loved ones that were found outside the dome, but this is the first time I've heard of a Bio-1 resident amongst them. I am so sorry to hear about your brother," she sincerely said.

Gregory sat back in his chair and frowned. "Yes, they did a good job covering *that* up. If word got out that a Bio-1 resident died in a seditious act, others in the aristocratic ranks would question authority."

Seeing that Gregory was sincere, Cheryl leaned forward onto her desk, and said, "so, tell me about your brother's diary."

Gregory smiled warily, and said, "my brother was concerned that geothermal drilling would lead to several nasty things. Among them were releasing of toxic gases into the bio-domes; inciting mars-quakes; and the scariest of all, a volcanic eruption of the Tharsis Bulge which would snuff out all of our lives."

Cheryl frowned, and asked, "anything else?"

"Yes," Gregory replied, "in his conversations with some of the scientists, he found out that our home world, Earth, was destroyed. That a year after we departed Earth the nations started a world-wide nuclear war. That this nuclear bombardment of the Earth shifted its orbital balance with the Moon. And that last year, the shift in the Earth-Moon balance increased Earth's gravitational pull on the Moon. That this increased gravitation caused the Moon to crash into Earth destroying whatever little life remained after the nuclear bombardment."

Tears welled in Cheryl's eyes. Of course, she knew of these events since her husband was an astrophysicist and he anguished over those newly discovered facts. And now, with the Earth uninhabitable and Mars on the possible brink of the same fate, she sat trembling.

Seeing Cheryl's face drain of its blood leaving an ashy skin color, Gregory stood, and said, "may I get you water?"

He did not wait for her to answer, instead he walked down the hall where he saw a water fountain, pulled out a paper cup from the dispenser, filled it with water, walked back to the office, and handed it to Cheryl.

41

Silently, she took the cup, sipped down its contents, then said in a low, even voice, "be careful who you say this to. Your life depends on it." With those words said, Cheryl placed the empty paper cup on her desk, leaned back in her chair, and silently observed Gregory.

Gregory sat back in his chair. With his head bowed, he anxiously wrung his hands. Frightened by pending doom, he desperately wanted someone to help him. He knew that none of the colonial managers would help; consequently, he knew that Cheryl was his last chance.

"A group of us are meeting in a few days concerning possible, future events," Cheryl finally said. "You can join us. I cannot tell you when and where due to security purposes. We will get in touch with you."

Getting this invitation to meet with the scientists from Bio-2 was more than Gregory had hoped for. And, to keep her confidence, he said, "I promise not to tell anyone about this meeting. However, I must let you know that I invited your son and his friends to tour Bio-1 tomorrow. And I promise you that I won't let our discussion leave this room."

CHAPTER 9

Just like before, Fly found himself exiting Bio-2 and transiting the connecting walkway to Bio-1. Unlike the time before, Fly was not alone. Both Otto and Alicia accompanied him to meet with Gregory.

"Please be nice to Gregory this time," Fly said to Otto.

Looking at the glances between the two guys, Alicia asked, "yeah, what's with you and Gregory? You guys seem to harbor a type of silent hate."

"I don't trust him," Otto said with a slight German accent.

As the three approached the guards at the entrance, Gregory popped his head out of the security door and motioned for them to enter. Because Gregory alerted the guards to his visitors ahead of time, they were able to walk right into Bio-1 without harassment.

Alicia immediately noticed the difference between Bio-1 and Bio-2. For one thing, their bio-dome was cramped with side-by-side shops, living quarters, and narrow walkways full of people. Bio-1, on the other hand, had few living quarters. These quarters were not boxy, cookie-cutter living-areas, but they were interspersed, tall, mushroom-shaped buildings with greenery hanging from balconies. Because the structures were mushroom-shaped: with a five-feet-in-diameter stem at the bottom that served as an elevator shaft and a bulbous four-story top filled with luxury apartments, there was more space on the ground for a greenspace. The greenspace covered the entire bottom of the dome. This area consisted of grass-covered rolling hills dotted with flowering and fir trees. Bisecting this greenspace, meandered a one-half, mile-wide stream which ran the entire diameter of the dome.

Looking in all directions, the three, Bio-2 occupants were mesmerized. They briefly heard how Bio-1 residents lived from friends and families who worked in service jobs in Bio-1, but to see the open spaces with glittering, mushroomed high-rises was more than they could have imagined.

"What is that?" Alicia asked while looking at a transparent, enclosed tube that wrapped around the entire dome.

While pointing at the structure something inside of it went by so fast that it was a blur.

Gregory smiled at her excitement, and replied, "that is our transport. It gets us around the city."

"You guys are too lazy to walk?" Otto scowled.

44

Feeling tension building between he and Otto, once again; Gregory pointed to a restaurant located by the river, and said, "well my friends, let's walk over there and grab lunch."

The four teens walked over to a one-story wooden eatery. Upon entering the eatery, Gregory saw how crowded it was. So, instead of sitting indoors, he led his company beyond the polished, wooden bar and sat at an outside table overlooking the river.

Once seated, a waiter was immediately at their table, and asked, "may I get you good folks some drinks while you look over the menu?"

Noticing that everyone ordered beer, Gregory said, "how about I order a couple of pitchers of beer?"

Seeing that Gregory was making a peace offering by ordering drinks for the group, Otto slightly smiled at him, and said, "okay, now you may call me friend."

Looking at the river which flowed under a simulated blue sky, Alicia took a deep breath. She loved watching the boats go by on the river and the birds flying across the domed sky.

"Birds?" She asked. "You have birds?"

Feeling awkward about living in luxury compared to the three other teens who worked for a living, Gregory replied, "yes. And there are fish in the river too. We are hoping that once the colony is expanded, all living spaces will be this way if not better."

After the pitchers of beer were placed on the table and the waiter recorded everyone's orders, Fly said, "you see Otto, if we win the talent competition, we could possible move to Bio-1."

Otto frowned, and said, "what if I don't want to live here?"

Fly shrugged his shoulders, and replied, "then you could go back to Earth for a visit. Trips to Earth are the second and third place prizes."

Again, Gregory felt uncomfortable. He knew that Earth was destroyed. He was now aware that the second and third prizes were a hoax. Gregory made a mental note to find out the reason behind the deception. Then remembering Fly's and Otto's performances earlier in the week, Gregory said, "the both of you are very talented. You two can very well win the talent competition."

Hearing a Bio-1 resident praise his music while knowing that most of the contest's judges would be drawn from those in power, Fly beamed.

As soon as their food was served, Heather joined them.

"Heather, what are you doing here?" Gregory asked his classmate.

After tossing back a head of strawberry blond hair, Heather asked "may I join you?"

"Well, I am here with my friends and...," Gregory began.

"Yeah, join us," Fly said as he pulled a chair from the unoccupied table next to them.

"You know her?" Gregory asked Fly.

"Heather spent the day at the drill site with me. She was very helpful," Fly replied.

"Heather? Helpful?" Gregory derided.

Heather narrowed her eyes as she stared at Gregory, and said, "just because my father is rich, doesn't mean that I don't aspire. Besides, I might one day be the head of the Utilities Ministry," she said with a slight British accent.

Before anyone said another word, the waiter appeared and recorded Heather's order. After the waiter walked away, Alicia smiled at Heather, and asked, "you want to head up the Utilities Ministry? Did you go to school for that?"

Heather sized up Alicia. Clearly, Alicia belonged to the lower classes—a working girl. Knowing that working people did not have the time to enjoy luxuries such as leisure time and higher education, she sympathetically smiled at the dark beauty that sat across from her. She remembered Alicia gave a lecture when her class toured the aquaponics plant. And unlike the leisure class, the working class did not attend classes of higher education, they apprenticed.

"Well, my uncle heads it up presently. And seeing that he is aging, I will possibly take over the reins," Heather replied.

"Nepotism," Otto said. "That practice is the downfall of most societies."

Fly, who sat next to Otto, nudged him.

Otto ignored Fly's warning to be civil.

"Well, don't you work in the same jobs as your parents?" Heather asked.

47

Otto jutted out his chin, and replied, "yes I do. I work on the drill team and my father supervises the power plant. That is the only career pathway for me. But what if I wanted to be the Minister of the Utilities? Huh? Is there some road for me to take that would lead to that career?"

Heather thought about this for a minute then replied, "yes, of course. The winners of the talent contest can live in Bio-1 and receive all the privileges its residents do. Those privileges include educational and job opportunities."

Otto's eyes narrowed as he stared at Heather. "These competitions have been going on for three years since we've colonized this planet and not one winner has come back to Bio-2 to let us know their accomplishments. Can you give me an example of an accomplished winner?"

Heather was flustered. She could not give Otto an example. "I will have to get back with you on that," she answered.

While Otto and Heather bantered, Gregory could not take his eyes off Alicia. From the first time he met her at the aquaponics' presentation and their subsequent meeting at Fly's house, he was smitten. He loved her classic Central American looks—the brown skin and silky, black hair. And, most of all, he loved her mind. She was smart and had no problems articulating her thoughts. Unlike the privileged girls that constantly surrounded him, Alicia had no desire to impress. Almost more than knowing about the circumstances behind his brother's death, he wanted to know Alicia. So, after Gregory gave his guests a quick tour of Bio-1 and they were on their way back to the entrance, he asked Alicia if he could see her again; claiming that he wanted to know more about the aquaponics plant. She accepted.

CHAPTER 10

Timing could not have been better for Gregory. On the same day as his meeting with the scientists of Bio-2, he and Alicia were to have lunch at Maria's Cantina. As usual, he arrived early. Instead of entering the establishment, he waited out front for Alicia. The front of the cantina—which was mostly a walkway—bustled with people. Mostly workers on their strict lunch breaks, these people had one mission—to grab a bite to eat before their lunch hour ended.

Elbow-to-elbow with the lunch crowd, Gregory was instantly aware of Bio-2's cramped living space. Again, he felt ashamed that his fellow citizens—through no choice of their own—were treated as a second class.

"There you are," Alicia said as she nearly bumped into Gregory.

Gregory smiled as he took in Alicia. Wearing her hair brushed into a top-notch and sporting form-fitting blue jeans topped with a loose-fitting, flower-print blouse; Alicia looked stunning. Forgetting his manners, Gregory silently gawked at his lovely lunch date.

"So, how about we get one of these outside tables," Alicia said while she pointed to a few empty tables located behind the establishment's roped-off area.

Gregory nodded and followed Alicia into the cantina where she asked the hostess for outside seating.

Upon seating, Alicia said after looking at her watch, "I only have forty-five minutes for lunch so we will have to talk while we eat. Now what do you want to know about the aquaponics plant?"

Before Gregory answered, a waiter appeared, recorded their orders, and deposited dessert menus.

Gregory gazed across the table at the Central American beauty. With her hair pulled back and wearing the loose-fitting cotton blouse, she looked out-worldly.

"Forgive me," Gregory said, "I just can't take my eyes off your blouse. The detailed embroidery is astounding!"

Pleased that he liked her blouse, Alicia smiled, and said, "this was my grandmother's blouse. I am glad you like it."

Getting a smile from Alicia, Gregory relaxed.

"My people originated from El Salvador. When we left Earth, I took little cloths with me. So, this blouse is one of my prize positions," she said while looking down at the short-sleeve white blouse accentuated by a deep-blue, lacy collar which hung loosely around her shoulders.

"El Salvador," Gregory repeated allowing the words to roll off his tongue.

"Like most of the Martian colonists, my parents were educated and were chosen to come to Mars. They worked for one of the colony's architects who resides in Bio-1. And, although my parents are science professionals, my grandmother—the original wearer of this blouse—was a shaman."

"Shaman?" Gregory asked.

"Yes, a person regarded as having access to, and influence in, the world of good and evil spirits. They help with healing and predict the future sometimes through dreams."

Gregory thought about this. He knew about the Siberian shamans. In tribal societies of Siberia and Central Asia shamanism always presented as a fundamental factor in religious life since the Bronze Age. He knew that although conventional Russians disapproved of them, many of the old traditions were secretly preserved. This intensified his interest.

After the waiter returned with their food, Gregory asked, "do you still have shamans in your family?"

Grabbing hold of her lunch—a two-fisted, hearty burrito filled with shredded beef, cheese, beans, and rice— Alicia took a bite, and replied, "although my grandmother was the last full-time shaman in my family, my mother has dabbled."

Using a knife and fork, Gregory cut into his burrito and took a bite. After swallowing down a mouthful, his eyes lit up.

Then forgoing proper manners, he picked up the entire burrito with both hands and bit off a sizable chunk.

Seeing the joyous look on Gregory's face as he chewed the flavorful bite, Alicia offered, "my mother is helping me decipher some of my recent, disturbing dreams."

With those words, Gregory muscled down the remaining mouthful, and attentively said, "I, too, have been having dreams that are uncharacteristic."

Alicia's eyes softened. "If you don't mind, tell me about your dream."

Eager to oblige, Gregory began, "it all starts when I find myself in an amazing valley surrounded by large, fragrant trees. The sun is shining brightly and there is a sparkling river flowing through the valley. And suddenly I am transported from the valley to a mountain top. This mountain top, or more so a plateau, is like none that I have ever seen. There are crystals everywhere. And they are not little crystals, but very large ones—some six-feet tall! These crystals are growing out of the ground. And—if this is not crazy enough—there are large crystal flowers floating in the air above my head! I stand there with the sun glistening through the crystals creating rainbows everywhere. Then an old man appears. This old man is holding the hand of a boy who is not more than three years old. The man—with flowing, white hair down to his back—wears only a loincloth. He looks like a shaman." Gregory paused.

At the mention of the man wearing a loincloth, Alicia held her breath. This was the same man in her dream who

53

transformed from an earthworm and into her grandfather. Wanting to hear more, Alicia asked, "and the boy? What did he look like?"

Gregory thought for a while, smiled, and replied, "the boy looked like no other. Although human, he looked like no race of people from the Earth. And when I looked into his eyes, I became frightened."

Curious about what could frighten a privileged person who probably never knew fear, Alicia asked, "what about his eyes frightened you?"

Recalling the strange boy and how he had difficulties maintaining his gaze, Gregory replied, "his eyes held infinity."

Intrigued, Alicia wanted to know more. However, before she asked another question, three chimes sounded. Upon hearing the chimes, she looked at her watch, retrieved money from her purse, placed it on the table and said, "lunchtime is over. Where did the time go? I am sorry we didn't get to discuss the aquaponics plant."

Disappointed they could not continue, Gregory also stood, and said, "let me get the bill."

Alicia shrugged her shoulders, and replied, "just pay what you owe. You can pick up the bill next time."

Pleased that there was going to be a *next time*, Gregory paid his bill, added a hefty tip, and joined Alicia where they exited the cantina. Once outside and on the busy walkway, Gregory secured a dinner date with Alicia for the following evening.

54

CHAPTER 11

Heather, once again, accompanied Fly to the drill site. While riding in the instrumentation vehicle with Fly, Heather was awestruck by the scenery. Looming ominously above Mars' hot, pink sky were its moons: *Phobos* and *Deimos*. Heather knew that these irregularly shaped moons were named after the Greek mythological twins who accompanied their father, Aries—the god of war—into battle. Although she knew that *Phobos* meant panic and fear and *Deimos* meant dread and terror, she did not know which was which.

While still looking at the moons that were looming in the daytime sky, Heather asked, "so, which is *Phobos* and which is *Deimos*?"

As an avid, amateur astronomer, Fly would have taken offense to such a question. However, not wanting to lose his possible fan-base, he replied, "the one on your left is *Phobos*." Satisfied with his answer, Heather remained silent. She then turned her focus from the sky to the landscape. As they rode from the domed colony to the drill site, Heather saw the ever present three volcanoes near them. And at a distant— located somewhere between the three volcanos—loomed Olympus Mons.

"These volcanoes are majestic!" Heather stated.

"They are amazing," Fly responded. From the first time Fly saw the volcanoes, they reminded him of the stars in the Orion constellation—its belt.

As the two silently drove toward the drill site, Fly remembered his father; a soft-spoken, medium-built man with thick, horn-rimmed glasses. Not only did Fly admire and love his father, but he hoped that one day he would become an astrophysicist like his father. His father taught him about the stars. Back on Earth, Fly spent many nights staring up at the stars with his father. His father enthusiastically named each visible star until Fly knew them all. However, after his father died on Mars, his hopes of following in his father's footsteps were dashed. For one thing, higher education was unavailable to Bio-2's occupants. And, another thing, he lost interest in the stars once his mentor was gone from his life. His interest in stargazing was replaced with knowing the answers to questions about his father's death. No one understood the scientists' mysterious deaths. Why were their bodies were found outside the bio-domes without protective equipment? Why was this group meeting? And, who let them out? To exit a bio-dome, someone must operate controls to let them out; no one admitted to doing so.

As they approached the drill site, Fly's attention turned to their present situation. "So, we are here," Fly said as he drove the vehicle to a stop.

Just as before, the two ensured that their environmental suits were in good, working order before they exited the vehicle. Mars' thin atmosphere—primarily composed of ninety-six percent carbon dioxide, almost three percent nitrogen, and almost two percent argon—was unbreathable. And, after exiting the vehicle, they took extra care during their journey around the vehicle due to Mars' gravitational pull. When in the bio-domes, the simulated gravity remained earth-like. On Mars' surface, however, the gravity was much less—which meant that minor exertions caused major movements.

After the two located themselves to the vehicle's instrument panel which contained the vital readings related to the drilling operations and its crew, Heather said, "I forgot to tell your friend, Otto, when we were suiting up for the trip that I looked into what happens to winners of the talent contest..."

Also interested in this information, Fly eagerly asked, "and, what did you find out?"

"I haven't found anything. Which is very odd."

"What do you mean? You haven't found anything."

"Once I got the names of the last winners and looked up their whereabouts, it seems that they just disappeared."

Fly looked over his instrument panel and noticed a slight increase in drill pressure.

"This is curious..." Heather began. However, before she continued speaking, she noticed that Fly immediately held his hand up which signaled a halt to the conversation.

"Drill site—come in," Fly said over his headset.

"Hey buddy. What is up," said Otto while carrying a casing to the drillers.

"Hey man, I noticed there is a slight pressure build-up on the drill bit."

"Roger that," Otto said, "I will let the supervisor know."

Then turning to Heather, Fly asked, "How could the contest winners have disappeared? They should have either obtained living quarters in Bio-1 or took a trip back to Earth."

"I do not know," Heather said pensively. Then with a glint in her eyes, she asked, "have you ever seen a rocket liftoff from the launch pad?"

Fly thought about this for a few moments, and replied, "no I haven't. But that means nothing since I am busy with day-to-day stuff."

CHAPTER 12

After lunch, Gregory leisurely walked to Bio-3.
Knowing that security cameras were ubiquitous and not
wanting to raise suspicion, he previously discussed with his
father about taking over the Ministry of Agriculture; thus,
receiving permission to become actively involved in the day-to-
day affairs of farming which included the aquaponics and
animal husbandry activities. Under this pretense, he freely
moved between bio-domes.

Upon entering Bio-3, he proceeded to the section
dedicated to animal husbandry where he was met by Alicia's
mother, Pythia.

Shaking Otto's hand with a dainty grip, Pythia said,
"Master Gregory, please come this way and I will give you a
tour of the ranch."

Although uncomfortable with the title Pythia bestowed upon him, Gregory nodded and kept up the performance for the cameras. The tour lasted approximately one hour as they moved from the various animal pens. Each pen contained at least one-hundred animals. Separated by species, there were pens containing sheep, cows, pigs, and chickens.

"So, you care for all of these animals?" Gregory asked.

Pythia nodded, and said, "I care for their medical needs. We have dozens of employees that feed and cleanup after them."

Realizing that living on Mars truly did take a village, Gregory nodded as he looked over the mass of living creatures.

"Now that we are done with the tour, would you like to join me for a late lunch?" Pythia asked.

Even though he was not hungry—since he had just had lunch with Alicia—Gregory smiled, and said, "thank you. That is perfect. I'm starved."

"We have food set up in the breakroom," Alicia said as she nodded her head in that direction.

When they entered the breakroom, Gregory noticed two other adults sitting around a table. Although it was not lunchtime, the middle of the table contained plates flowing with sandwiches, fruits, and potato chips. Gregory nodded at the other individuals, filled a plate full of food, and sat next to Pythia.

"No cameras here," said a man in his forties boasting a slight German accent.

"Pardon my manners," said Pythia. "Let me introduce you to our group. This gentleman," she said nodding to the broad man across from them, "is Gunther. You may have met his son, Otto." Next, she nodded at the slender African American woman sitting next to Gunther, and said, "I believe you already know Cheryl."

Cheryl nodded at Gregory.

"So, what is your interest here, young man?" Gunther asked.

Gregory leveled Gunther a non-threatening stare. He noticed Gunther's broad shoulders, thick head of hair, and strong jaw; he was almost the spitting image of Otto. Realizing there was no room for pleasantries, Gregory came to the point, and said, "after my brother, Yuri, died —along with a few of the scientists—I found his diary. In the diary, Yuri raised many questions. The question that I found particularly disturbing was the one concerning deep, geothermal drilling."

Gunther's eyes narrowed. "What did he question about it?"

"He wondered if it would set off earthquakes, rather, Mars-quakes. Quakes that followed earth-practices like *Fracking*?"

In the ensuing silence, Gregory found himself locked in a gripping stare with Gunther.

"Go on," Pythia softly encouraged.

"I know that this is the only planet that we can live on. Yuri detailed the destruction of Earth. I also know that our colony sits on the Tharsis Bulge for geothermal energy purposes. If we trigger Mars-quakes by drilling deep within the planet, we might cause a mega quake."

"Of course," began Gunther, "we have raised these issues to the Ministry of Energy. Although they acknowledged our concerns, they did nothing about them. All they care about is energy production for colonial expansion."

Gregory nodded in sympathy, and said, "when a society is ruled by aristocratic businessmen, all science goes out the window. They always want more studies into the matter while hoping it will go away."

"And, they want hard proof," Cheryl added. "Unfortunately, our science hasn't advanced enough to reasonably predict earthquakes."

Gunther's eyes glassed over. He said in a softer voice, "science and proof threaten them. Upon being threatened, they remove the threat. Your brother, my wife, and both Cheryl- and Pythia's husbands threatened them. And now they are all dead."

With those words, the four simultaneously bowed their heads while remembering their loved ones.

After moments of silence, Pythia soberly asked the group, "what can we do? How can we protect our living loved-ones?"

Cheryl shook her head, and replied, "I don't know what to do. We have no scientific proof that these practices will lead to a catastrophe."

"Maybe not *scientific* proof," Pythia began, "but we do have *anecdotal* happenings."

62

Gunther, the consummate engineer, sighed. Although he only believed in science that was reproducible through numbers and equations, he sat silent and listened.

"Anecdotal proof?" Cheryl asked.

"Yes," Pythia replied. "My daughter has had a series of recurring dreams. And, before you dismiss me, you should hear me out." She paused and looked around the table. When there was no sign of stopping her, she continued, "as you know, I am not only a veterinarian, but I also hail from a long line of Mayan shamans. In that tradition, we take dreams seriously; especially ones that reoccur resulting with lack of sleep."

Pythia paused and looked at Gregory. When she saw that he eagerly wanted her to continue, she said, "Alicia's dreams are centered around earthquakes and catastrophic destruction. A destruction so devastating that everyone in the colony will die."

"When is this catastrophe supposed to happen?" Gregory asked.

Pythia shrugged her shoulders, and replied, "it could happen today, tomorrow, or in decades from now. These dreams only serve as a warning."

Gunther, the head of the power plant, shook his head. In the past, he would have been furious of such a notion, however, knowing what this group has been through, he lessened his anger, and said, "I am afraid that dreams won't compute with the Ministry of Energy as proof."

Silence gripped the group.

63

Gregory's eyes lit up as he looked at Pythia, and asked, "you said you had anecdotal happenings? So, are there other things?"

Pythia nodded, and replied, "again, this is not scientific proof. But several of our animals have fallen ill."

"I don't understand," Gunther said. "What does that have to do with Mars-quakes?"

Cheryl, slowly nodded her head, and asked, "are their illnesses physical or psychological?"

"After running them through a series of tests, I could not find anything physically wrong with these animals. Therefore, their illnesses must be psychological."

Although a hardcore geophysicist, Cheryl was aware of anecdotal evidence linking animal behavior to earthquakes, she explained, "anecdotal evidence abounds of animals, fish, birds, reptiles, and insects exhibiting strange behaviors anywhere from weeks to seconds before an earthquake. However consistent and reliable, behavior prior to seismic events, and a mechanism explaining how it could work, still eludes us. Even though we westerners did not pursue this line of study, Chinese and Japanese scientists did."

"What did they study?" Gregory asked.

Getting into her lecturing mode, Cheryl replied, "well there are two types of waves that we are concerned with when there is an earthquake; they are P and S waves. The P wave, or primary wave, is the fastest kind of seismic wave, and, consequently, the first to arrive at a seismic station. The P wave can move through solid rock and fluid, like water or the liquid layers of the earth. It pushes and pulls the rock it moves through just like sound waves push and pull the air. Have you ever heard a big clap of thunder and heard the windows rattle at the same time? The windows rattle because the sound waves were pushing and pulling on the window glass much like P waves push and pull-on rock. Sometimes animals can hear the P waves of an earthquake. Dogs, for instance, commonly begin barking hysterically just before an earthquake hits. Usually, people can only feel the bump and rattle of these waves."

Now, following the science of the conversation, Gunther asked, "what about the S wave?"

Glad that she got Gunther's attention, Cheryl replied, "the S wave, or secondary wave, is the second wave you feel in an earthquake. An S wave is slower than a P wave and can only move through solid rock, not through any liquid medium. It is this property of S waves that led seismologists to conclude that the Earth's outer core is a liquid. The S waves move rock particles up and down, or side-to-side which is perpendicular to the direction in which the wave is traveling. Secondary waves are the second seismic wave to arrive at any location after an earthquake, though they start at the same time as primary waves. Secondary waves travel through Earth's interior at about half the speed of primary waves. As they pass through a material, the material's particles are shaken up and down or from side to side. Secondary waves rock small buildings back and forth as they pass."

"So, secondary waves cause the earthquake destruction," Gunther concluded.

Cheryl nodded.

"So, you are saying that the animals may be feeling these waves already traveling through Mars' subsurface?" Pythia asked.

Cheryl nodded.

For the first time since he sat at the adult table, Gregory looked frightened. "So, what I am hearing between the two of you ladies is that there is a catastrophic event—possibly a Mars-quake—about to happen. And this may take place any second now!"

Seeing the panic look on everyone's faces, Cheryl said, "not exactly. We don't quite know much about Mars' subsurface."

"What about the sick animals?" Gregory asked.

"Although we do not know much about Mars' subsurface, by the large, looming volcanos in our backyard, we do know that Mars was once volcanically active. So, there still may be tremors from magma chambers beneath the surface which may not cause a catastrophe."

Still filled with a hint of fright, Gregory asked, "but, are not fracking, earthquakes, and volcanos related? Could we be causing a catastrophic Mars-quake followed by a massive volcanic eruption?"

Cheryl remained silent.

"You have seismometers? Those instruments that measure subsurface activities. Yes?" Gunther asked Cheryl.

Cheryl nodded.

66

"Are there any curious readings that might coincide with the sick animals?"

Cheryl looked at Pythia, and said, "maybe we can get together and analyze these data."

Pythia agreed.

"What if we find that these data coincide?" Gregory asked.

Again, everyone remained silent. They knew that if this was the case, then they were doomed! Everyone at the table knew that in the horrific scenario where the drilling leads to Mars-quakes and a massive volcanic eruption that they had nowhere to go.

Knowing this, Gregory still had to ask, "can we survive a massive volcanic eruption? Can our bio-domes save us from dying?"

Gunther shook his head, and replied, "these bio-domes were constructed to save us from minor meteor strikes. We located our colony on the Tharsis Bulge, to benefit from the geothermal energy beneath this surface. We thought only about our immediate survival needs. We foolishly assumed that these volcanos were dormant. We did not think about future catastrophic events. So, if Olympus Mons or either of the other three volcanos erupt, our bio-domes will be obliterated by the pyroclastic blast."

Silently, everyone knew that Gunther was correct.

"I know that Earth is destroyed, so we can't go back there. But can we ready our spaceships and voyage to a semi-habitable moon—say Saturn's Titan or Jupiter's Europa?" Gregory pleadingly asked.

Initially, Gunther did not like Gregory for many reasons. For one, the long-standing hatred between Russia and Germany was ingrained in his brain. And, most important, although he had no proof, he blamed the aristocrats in Bio-1 for his wife's death; particularly, Gregory's father. However, now knowing that Gregory's brother was among those found dead outside of Bio-3, he softened towards the young man. And, seeing panic washed across Gregory's face reminded him of his son, Otto. He felt sympathy for the boy.

So, shaking his head, once again, Gunther said in a softer tone, "those are great ideas. You should have been on the colony's planning team," he said with a smile and a hint of a wink to Gregory. "However, the planning team prided itself on making spacecrafts that were recyclable."

Pythia asked, "recyclable? I don't quite understand."

Gunther nodded, and explained, "yes, recyclable. Every part of our spaceships from their outer hull to the nuts and bolts, which held them together, were used to build our bio-domes. Presently, there are not any spaceships. The hope was that after we got here, we would build more."

"And?" Cheryl asked.

"And" Gunther said, "when the powers-to-be learned that Earth was rendered uninhabitable, building spaceships was put on hold. The emphasis then was the expansion of our living, working, and relaxation spaces by creating additional bio-domes."

68

Cheryl's eyes glassed over. "We are doomed," she concluded.

With Cheryl's words sinking in, Gregory bowed his head in silence. Looking at the breakroom's table, he searched his mind for something, anything! Instantly, he brightened up and looked around the table at the others whose faces were sadden with teary eyes. And smiling, he asked, "what about the South Dakota colony?"

CHAPTER 13

Heather liked Fly. He was unlike her friends in Bio-1. Not only did he have a job, but he also had a hobby. She loved his music. During their ride to the drill site, Fly rapped several of his original lyrics. As a child, Heather wanted for nothing. She was born to one of London's *old-money* families. She was consistently surrounded by tutors and maids who catered to her every impulse. Her friends were children of the wealthiest families from all over the globe—some of whom colonized Mars. However, after listening to Fly's raps about the trials and tribulations of *common people*, she felt hollow. She could not quite explain the emptiness; but she knew that filling it would reignite her life. She wanted to know more about Fly.

While Fly was softly rapping as he looked over the instrument panel, Heather asked, "so, where did you grow up?"

"Brooklyn, New York," Fly replied while fondly remembering the brownstone, three-bedroom home in Brooklyn.

"Brooklyn?" She said with a frown. The only thing she knew about Brooklyn was crime and dirt. However, she did love New York's Broadway district with all the cutting-edge theatrical plays; Times Square with its gilts and glitter; and the shopping districts such as SOHO and NOHO.

Fly loved Brooklyn. Particularly, he loved the emergence of humanity the insane hustle and bustle of every type of human being possible. He loved the eateries where most restaurants were owned by actual residents. He loved eating out at his father's favorite Cuban café that served yellow rice, beans, and shredded meat. He loved going on walks with his mother across the Brooklyn Bridge; looking over the rails and into the harbor to catch a peak of the Statue of Liberty. And he loved his public school and all his friends. All of this ended when his parents were recruited by an aerospace firm located in San Diego, California. And, although San Diego was impressive with its climate, beaches, and laidback vibe, he missed the hustle, bustle, and change of seasons that Brooklyn had to offer. And now, when the firm secretly relocated them to Mars where his life was completely uprooted, he missed Brooklyn even more. Thinking about his early childhood while growing up in Brooklyn, Fly slipped into a rap from his music idol, *Jay-Z*.

Listening to the lyrics, Heather was shocked by the explicit, raw feelings, and asked, "when did you write that one?"

Fly stopped rapping, let out a hearty laugh, and said, "I can only wish that my lyrics would sound so good. No, that is one of *Jay-Z's* amazing raps."

By the emphasis Fly put on the name: *Jay-Z*, Heather knew that she should have heard of the musician; yet she did not and was silent. Hiding her ignorance through silence, Heather decided to switch the subject. However, before she had a chance to think up anything to say, Fly cried out, "holy shit!"

Everything following his exclamation was a blur to Heather. In a daze, Heather watched as Fly moved his hands across the instrument panel in a panic. Red throbbing lights filled the panel. As some lights throbbed and flashed, other lights shut off completely.

"What's happening?" Heather asked.

"Get in the vehicle," he ordered. "We need to get to the drill rig!"

Heather did as she was told and quickly hopped into the vehicle. Although they were only two-hundred yards from the rig, it seemed like miles. Heather's heart raced as she watched Fly. Besides driving at top speeds through Mars' dusty, dry, loose surface; he pounded on the vehicle's dashboard. With every hit of the dashboard, Fly subconsciously screamed an expletive.

72

When they came upon the rig and after the vehicle stopped, Fly ordered Heather to remain inside. He saw that at the immediate rig site that all the crew were motionlessly lying down on the dusty ground and that their environmental suits were compromised. And approximately twenty feet from the rig-site, next to a pipe casing lay the only life sign that appeared on his instrument panel. It was his friend, Otto.

Racing to Otto's side, he saw that the environmental suit was still intact. Instinctively, Fly reached under his downed friend's shoulders and frantically pulled him back to the vehicle. After entering the vehicle, Fly instructed Heather to remove Otto's headgear so that he could breathe the vehicle's oxygenated air.

While Heather removed Otto's headgear, she asked, "what about the others."

Fly shook his head as he sped the vehicle back to Bio-3, and softly said, "it is too late for them."

While recklessly driving at top speeds, Fly observed several, small, dust tornadoes ahead. Normally, he would mentally calculate the directions of these dust devils and plan a path around them, but all he could think of was getting Otto safely home.

"I think he is not breathing," said Heather from the compartment behind the two seats.

Panicked, Fly screamed to Heather, "do you know first aid?"

Tears rolled down Heather's face as she shook her head, and said, "no, I…"

73

Fly put the vehicle on autopilot, removed his helmet, and joined Heather in the back compartment. As he knelt next to Otto, he asked Heather, "do you know how to drive?"

Once again, Heather shook her head, and said, "I always had a chauffeur, I…I,"

Fly nodded at the driver's seat, and ordered, "take the driver's seat. The vehicle is in autopilot. All you have to do is try to avoid the dust storms ahead of us."

Heather froze. She felt completely useless.

While Fly secured the first-aid kit, Heather stood perfectly still.

Upon returning to Otto's side, he said to Heather, "you can do this. Take a few deep breaths and go!"

Both charged and encouraged by Fly's words, Heather leapt into the driver's seat.

Fly inventoried his downed friend and noticed that he was indeed breathing slow, shallow breaths. He observed that Otto's face was pale, and his skin was clammy. Even though this alarmed him, he became even more alarmed by the slow deterioration of Otto's environmental suit. When he first grabbed Otto from the site, his suit looked normal. However slightly, while his friend laid on the back-compartment's floor, holes were visible on the suit—and these holes were getting larger!

"I see Bio-3 up ahead," Heather called to Fly. But just as she said that the vehicle became engulfed in a dust storm.

"What do I do? What do I do? I can't see anything anymore!" Heather shouted.

74

"Hold on Heather," Fly replied.

Returning his attention back to Otto, Fly opened the first aid kit, retrieved a scissor, and steadily began cutting Otto's environmental suit. He worked as quickly as possible to peel away the suit. "There must have been some sort of acid that they released during the drilling," he said to himself.

After Otto was stripped of his environmental suit, Fly removed his own suit in case the acid was accidentally transferable. Then, seeing that Otto was stable, he instructed Heather to come to the back compartment and remove her suit.

Fly looked into Heather's terrified face, and said, "he is stable. I want you to stay back here and watch him. Let me know if there is any change in his condition."

Immediately after Fly gained control of the vehicle, he assessed their situation. Although he could not see anything out of the vehicle's window due to the swirling, red dust; he knew by the instrument readings that they were still on course for Bio-3. So, he radioed Bio-3, let them know there was an emergency and that he needed to drive directly into the hangar since no one in the vehicle was wearing environmental suits.

CHAPTER 14

"What about the South Dakota colony?" Gregory asked again as he looked at everyone around the breakroom's table.

Vaguely, the scientists around the table remembered talk of a group of anarchists from South Dakota.

"I remember hearing about a group of radicals residing in South Dakota. I vaguely remember hearing that they were overtaken by the United States government and they all died," Gunther said. "But what does that have to do with our situation?"

"They weren't anarchists," Pythia said. "Several years ago, while living on Earth, there was talk amongst the Central American Mayans about a spiritual energy, if you will, that was drawing people to South Dakota. And not just the Mayans; many Native American tribes felt this energy."

"I also heard that they weren't radicals," Cheryl agreed. "I heard talk amongst many scientists that a South Dakota group was making major advances in science. And even though they lived in seemingly primitive conditions in the Black Hills, their scientific advances were leaps and bounds above our present knowledge."

Energized that both Cheryl- and Pythia's accounts of the South Dakota colony confirmed his brother's suspicions, Gregory said, "in my brother's diary, he spoke about this colony. They were approximately two-thousand people from all walks of life and all different talents. They were scientists, intellectuals, carpenters, shamans, teachers, farmers, and many others. But, incredible as this seems, some were very old souls. Souls that have fought against oppression throughout thousands of years."

Pythia smiled, and asked, "you are saying that some of these people had past lives?"

Gregory nodded, and replied, "yes, all of them had past lives, however, few remembered them. But, if Yuri's journal is correct, that wasn't the most incredible thing."

Intrigued, Cheryl said, "we would be a formidable race of creatures if we had previous lives and built our future on past experiences."

"What was the most incredible thing about this society?" Gunther asked.

"Their children," Gregory replied. "The children of these old souls retained the knowledge of thousands of years. They were incredible."

Anger washed over Gunther's face, and he asked, "what does this fantasy have to do with us?"

Gregory leveled Gunther a sincere look, and replied, "if the stories are true, then they have everything to do with us. According to Yuri's diary, this colony was not wiped out by the United States government. They escaped in their scientifically-advanced spaceship."

Gunther thought about this for a while. Knowing that space-travel was indeed possible, he asked, "to where did they escape? They clearly aren't on Mars with us."

Gregory shrugged his shoulders, and replied, "I don't know where they are."

Cheryl leaned forward, and added, "my Charles told me that just before the Moon crashed into Earth, he and other astrophysicists, who were monitoring the Earth's sky, saw what they believed were several massive spaceships leaving Earth."

They all thought about this.

"Yuri," Gregory said with excitement, "he too saw this with his own telescope. That is written in his diary!"

As an engineer, Gunther dealt in facts. Before, he would never entertain fantastical thinking as real. However, since his now dead astrophysicist wife, Greta, told him about her own suspicions concerning other spaceships in Earth's orbit just before the massive catastrophe, he engaged seriously with everyone around the table, and stated, "if there are Earthlings, other than us that survived the destruction of our beloved, home planet, then what can we do? How can we contact them?"

"We can create a beacon," Gregory replied.

"Yes," Pythia eagerly added, "a distress call."

For the first time tension left Gunther's face, he smiled, and nodded, "we could do that."

However, before anyone spoke another word a blaring alarm sounded and a voice over the loudspeaker announced, "there is an emergency at the drill site!"

The four quickly rose from the table and headed to the energy plant's control room.

CHAPTER 15

Normally, travel time from Bio-3's breakroom to the power plant's control room took about a half an hour. However, with Gunther in the lead—his feet walking as fast as his heart pumping—the four arrived at the control room in less than ten minutes. Except for Pythia, the group had either a child or friend at the drill site. After entering the control room, Gunther assessed the situation.

"Allow the vehicle to enter the high-bay," Gunther instructed the workers in the high-bay area over his headset. "After the vehicle is in, secure the door and make sure that the environment is safe so they can breathe the air."

Gunther, who thought only of his son's safety, was reminded that Cheryl's son was also in potential danger. Looking into Cheryl's frightened eyes, Gunther said, "let's go to the high-bay area."

The group reached the high-bay area in less than five minutes. Through a window that led to the inner-bay area they saw the motionless vehicle.

"Fly!" Cheryl shouted as she reached for the door.

Gunther grabbed her hand, pulled her back, and said, "no, you can't go in there. We must wait until the environment is suitable."

Although it took only two minutes, it seemed like hours until the group entered the high-bay area.

Cheryl's heart calmed somewhat when she saw Fly exit the vehicle. However, Gunther's heart sank when he saw no sign of Otto.

Seeing the approaching group, Fly said, "Otto is inside the vehicle. He needs medical attention."

Simultaneously, as Heather exited the vehicle, Gunther entered and was immediately at his unconscious son's side.

"We need a doctor here!" Fly yelled out.

Before medic personnel appeared, Gunther exited the vehicle and loomed over Fly. "What happened?" He asked.

Even though Fly's eyes were nearly glazed over in shock, he responded, "I don't know. I received a pressure buildup on my monitors. I relayed the reading to the drill site. Then within minutes, alarms sounded concerning both the crew's environmental suits and their vital readings."

Gunther noticed Fly's rapid breathing and glassy eyes, and said calmly, "slow down, son."

But Fly could not slow down. He was still in a panic mode. "When I saw the alarming readings, I sped to the site.

81

By the time I got there, the only one with biomctrics was Otto. I dragged him from the site and sped back. While speeding back, I saw that Otto's environmental suit was disintegrating. So, I immediately removed his suit. And, just in case ours were also contaminated from contact with Otto's, we removed ours." He said with a nod over to Heather.

As Fly fell silent and lowered his head, he saw that the medics were on site and hoisting Otto onto a stretcher. "Please be okay, buddy," Fly said as the medics were about to wheel Otto away on a gurney.

Gunther put a hand on Fly's shoulder, and said, "listen, son. I want you and Heather to go with Otto to sickbay. I want you two checked out by the medics."

With her hand on Fly's other shoulder, Cheryl said to Gunther, "I will take them there." Then knowing that Gunther needed to recover the rest of the drill crew and conduct an immediate investigation, Cheryl added, "I will stay at Otto's side and keep you informed."

Torn between being with his son and conducting his official duties, Gunther was silent.

Cheryl touched his hand, looked him in the eyes, and said, "you need to find out what happened. I will take care of our children."

Both Cheryl and Gunther shared a special bond. When their spouses were found dead outside of the bio-dome, they learned to depend upon each other for emotional support; to trust each other.

82

After taking a deep breath, Gunther silently nodded and departed to the control room to conduct the investigation.

CHAPTER 16

One could hear a pin drop in sickbay. Eight biomedical beds lined the length of the rectangular room. Each bed was equipped with a stool next to it and a readout screen directly above the bed. Three of the eight beds were occupied with Otto, Fly, and Heather. In the far corner, Cheryl and Gregory huddled together. Neither of them said a word. They just watched while Fly, Otto, and Heather were being examined.

While intently looking at the readout screens above both Fly- and Heather's biomedical beds, Cheryl discerned that their readings were normal; even though Fly's heart rate was slightly high.

"We're okay, Mom," Fly said as he and Heather walked toward Cheryl and Gregory.

Cheryl embraced her son, kissed his cheek, and said, "I love you so much, baby."

Fly held onto his mom for a few seconds. Then looking back at Otto, he said, "I hope my buddy is fine. I don't know…"

Before he finished his sentence, he saw that Otto's readouts were returning to normal levels. He raced to Otto's bedside to see that his friend had regained consciousness.

"Hey, buddy," Fly said with knitted eyebrows.

Lethargically, Otto blinked. When he tried to raise up on his elbows, the doctor gently warned, "son, you are not out of the woods yet."

Feeling lightheaded, Otto laid back down, looked up into Fly's anxious eyes, and asked, "what happened? Last thing I remember is that I was retrieving an additional casing for the well and now I am here. Did something happen to my environmental suit? Did I have an oxygen leak?"

Feeling his mother's hand squeeze his shoulder, Fly fell silent.

Cheryl leaned down and kissed Otto on the cheek. She then looked at the doctor, and suggested, "we should let Otto rest. Shouldn't we?"

The doctor nodded while inserting a needle full of sedatives into a tube which hung from a bag of revitalizing fluids.

As Otto quickly succumbed to the sedative and slowly closed his eyes, the doctor said to Fly, "we will let you talk

85

after he rests. And I want you two to also take it easy," he said to Fly and Heather.

After Fly was convinced that his friend was out of danger, he nodded, and said to the group, "let's let Otto rest."

As they walked out of sickbay, Gregory gently asked Fly, "do you know what happened at the drill site?"

With the group of four positioned in the hall outside of sickbay, Fly responded, "during drilling, there was a pressure buildup at the drill bit. And, just as quickly as the pressure increased, it decreased."

"What do you mean decreased?" Cheryl asked.

Frustratingly, Fly shook his head, and answered, "I mean that the pressure gage went to zero!"

Thinking geologically, Cheryl imagined a geologic egg; a hard surface on the outside followed by a soft surface—or a void—on the inside. Then as a second thought, she imagined that inside was not an empty void. 'It was filled with some dangerous gas,' she thought to herself. And, since she and other scientists knew nothing about Mars' subsurface, a geologic egg was the best image she could think of.

Cheryl looked at each of the three teenagers, and said, "it has been a long day for you guys. You should go home and relax."

Everyone agreed.

Upon departure, Cheryl radioed Gunther. First, she let him know that Otto was stable and resting. Next, she said that she wanted to talk to him about the accident investigation; she might have some insights.

CHAPTER 17

Sitting on a picnic blanket, next to Gregory, Alicia watched boats as they sailed by on Bio-1's river. In true regatta fashion, these ten sailboats competitively floated in a line with their colorful spinnakers leading the way. The blue water beneath the boats reflected the simulated, blue earth-sky. Although Alicia was impressed by the blue sky, she was equally impressed by the warmth she felt from the holographic sun which gingerly peaked out from similar holographic puffy clouds.

Laying on her back with her eyes now closed, Alicia felt the sun on her face. Without opening her eyes, she sighed, and said, "I could really get used to this."

Gregory smiled at the beauty who languished next to him. He knew that her days were mostly filled with work and all out tedium. He suddenly wanted to lavish her in his world.

"My family is hosting a party tomorrow evening; and I would love it if you were my guest."

Alicia opened her eyes, propped up on her elbows, looked at Gregory, and asked, "a party?"

Pleadingly looking into her eyes, Gregory explained, "yes. The party is in celebration of our colony's third year of existence."

Alicia—along with everyone in Bio-2—celebrated the birth of the Martian colony every year. The Bio-2 celebration consisted of outdoor cookouts, parades, and sporting events. She knew that Bio-1's inhabitants also recognized this yearly event, but never knew how it was celebrated. Eagerly, she said, "I would love to be your guest."

Happy that Alicia agreed to accompany him, Gregory simply stared at her with a humble smile on his face.

Unaccustomed to this type of attention, Alicia shyly redirected her gaze back to the regatta. After a few moments of silence, she said, "I was wondering what type of education you Bio-1 students get."

Shaken from musing about their next date, Gregory asked, "what do you mean?"

This question has always been in the back of Alicia's mind. She knew that education in Bio-2 focused on hospitality and technical training, which meant once a student graduated from high school, they received further training to serve inhabitants in Bio-1 by homemaking—cooking, cleaning, and dressmaking—, or maintaining and operating the power and aquaponics plants, or working in animal husbandry and food processing plants.

"What I mean is when students in Bio-1 graduate from high school, do they get any further education?"

"Of course," he answered. "Presently, we can choose several managerial careers."

"Like Heather who wants to head up the Utilities Ministry?"

Gregory nodded.

"What about science?" Alicia asked.

Gregory thought long on this question. As far as he knew, there were not any major scientific courses.

"The only other choice we have after graduating from high school is to apprentice with a medical professional."

With those words, the two fell silent.

"How can we expand our colony if we don't have scientists and engineers to think the expansion through?" Alicia asked.

Gregory was silent.

"And why do we have so many doctors?"

Not knowing that answer either, Gregory shook his head in despair.

"It seems to me," said Alicia, "that the colony's planning was somewhat shortsighted."

Gregory agreed. While nodding, he said, "maybe we can come up with a *future-forward* plan and present it to our leaders."

Alicia shrugged her shoulders, and said, "I would like that."

With those questions off her mind, Alicia laid back on the blanket. Staring at the holographic clouds that floated across the simulated blue skies, she relaxed and thought about her recent dream. In a softer tone, she said, "I had a dream last night."

Now lying on the blanket on his side with his head propped upon a bended arm, Gregory said, "tell me about it."

"I am not sure if it was triggered by your dream, but the same boy was in mine. He looked like no child that I had ever seen before: dark skin, green eyes, and a most hypnotic smile."

Eagerly nodding, Gregory said, "that's him! However, I don't remember telling you those details about the boy."

"He led me to a valley with a crystal-clear stream," she continued. "The sun was shining. I could feel the sun's warmth wrapping around my body. And not a short distance from the stream was a stand of flowering trees. Oh, the fragrance! And, beyond the flowering trees was a mountain of evergreen trees. And, on top of the mountain I could see crystals floating in the air."

Gregory was electrified with chills. Those were the same crystals from his dream.

"When the sun shone on the crystals, they behaved like optical prisms and emitted every color of the rainbow," Alicia continued. "Not only were my senses on overload by feeling the sun's warmth, smelling the aromatic flowers, and seeing the impossibly floating crystals emitting wonderfully sharp colors; but my spirit was peacefully at rest. I felt hope."

Gregory remained silent.

A serene smile graced Alicia's face. She turned on her side, stared deeply into Gregory's eyes, and said, "and the boy. When he held my hand and looked into my eyes, I felt infinite."

"That's exactly how I felt when I looked into his eyes," said Gregory.

Alicia's smile now turned into a full out laugh when she asked, "do you think that someone is trying to tell us something?"

Puzzled, Gregory answered her question with other questions, and asked, "like what? What are they trying to tell us? And who are *they*?"

After a few moments of silence, Alicia said, "I have had previous dreams; dreams that terrified me to my core. Those dreams were of destruction and death. But this one was more of hope for a future. I believe that something is about to happen."

"What is about to happen?"

Alicia shrugged her shoulders, and replied, "I don't know. But I am getting the feeling that life, as we know it, is about to change."

CHAPTER 18

Gunther strolled briskly through the power plant with the Minister of Utilities at his side. Clive Barrister, who is also Heather's uncle, hailed from a powerful, *old-money* family in England. As he walked next to the muscular Gunther, he could barely keep pace. Clive's rotund physique turned his hurried walk into an awkward waddle.

Stopping mid-stride, Clive breathlessly asked, "how much farther is your conference room?"

Gunther detested aristocrats. Growing up in a poor town in Germany, Gunther watched both his mother and father struggle just to keep food on the table. Many times, when their paychecks were not enough to make ends meet, his mother took him along with her to their neighborhood church where he carried home a cardboard box filled with donated can-goods.

As a young adult, he received a partial scholarship to the nation's top engineering school. He was thankful that class work was easy for him because he worked at two, part-time jobs to afford food and clothes. So, seeing this aristocrat struggle to walk, made him inwardly smile.

"The conference room is just over there," Gunther replied as he spitefully picked up the pace.

When they entered the conference room, both Fly and Heather were already there and seated at the table. As Clive breathlessly flopped into a chair across from the two, Gunther nodded towards a platter full of pastries located in the middle of the table, and said, "help yourself."

Immediately standing, Heather asked, "uncle, may I pour you coffee?"

Clive looked like a pumpkin. He had an unusually large head with surprisingly youthful, blue eyes. He scrunched his nose, and replied, "dear Heather, you know that a proper gentleman drinks nothing but tea."

"We have tea in the kitchen. Look in the left cabinet on the upper shelf," Gunther said as he nodded his head towards an opened door.

While Heather disappeared through the doorway, Clive retrieved a doughnut from the pastry tray.

"Who is this fellow?" Clive asked with a nod in Fly's direction.

Before Gunther answered, Heather returned with a steaming-hot cup of tea for her uncle.

93

"This is Fly, he is a member of the drill crew," Gunther replied.

Fly nodded.

"Explain to me what happened at the drill site, young man," Clive demanded.

"Mr. Barrister," Fly began, "the drill crew: Otto, Andy, Bobby, Carlos, and six others; had drilled about one-hundred and fifty feet below the surface when the drill bit hit a harder surface. At that point, the gage read increased pressure at the drill bit. I informed them over my communication's device that this was happening. And as soon as I saw the pressure increase, it suddenly decreased. It was as if the drill bit had penetrated an air bubble."

"Well, which is it, young man!" Clive demanded. "Was there increased pressure or decreased pressure? He is nothing but a child," Clive said now turning his attention to Gunther. "Why was he in charge of such an important part of the operation?"

Somewhat raddled, Fly looked to Gunther.

"I can assure you, Mr. Barrister, that Fly is highly competent. And, to answer your question, there was increased pressure followed by sudden decreased pressure which indicates that the drill bit penetrated a hard surface which enclosed a toxic substance. Upon penetrating the hard surface, a toxic substance rushed up the well engulfing everyone near the drill site."

"Was it an acid?" Heather timidly asked.

Gunther nodded, and said, "something like that. We had it analyzed and it is like nothing we have seen before. The second it contacts a surface, it disintegrates it."

"So, the drill crew was at fault!" Clive accused.

Gunther did all he could to control his temper; he clinched his teeth so tightly that his jaw muscles were clearly visible. "That crew was the best crew there is. They are responsible for the geothermal heating and cooling that this colony so mindlessly enjoys. They were *not* at fault. They followed procedures to the letter!"

Although interested in Gunther's defense of the drill crew, Heather could not take her eyes off her uncle's face. Something was out of place. After a few observations, she noticed that her uncle's eye color was all wrong. Before, he had hazel eyes. And he always wore thick, horn-rimmed glasses. Now, his eyes were a startling blue. And he wore no glasses.

"Uncle," Heather said, "I was there, and everyone was extremely professional. No one was at fault."

Ignoring Heather's defense of the drill crew, Clive asked, "when can operations begin? We must be on schedule so that the settlement's expansion can continue."

Gunther became angry at Clive's unsympathetic question. He stood, loomed over the plump minister, and said, "I have nine dead crewmen! My son is in sickbay recovering from his injuries. Their environmental suits are deteriorated. We do not quite know what happened at that site. We need to investigate further so that this doesn't happen again."

"When can operations continue?" Clive rigidly demanded.

"I am not sending anyone to drill until we investigate the site. An investigation means we need to use remote sensing instruments to thoroughly map the subsurface."

Clive's stout face reddened. Like a vicious dog with his jaw locked shut after sinking his teeth into a piece of raw meat, Clive would not let go. "When can operations continue?" Clive insisted.

Knowing that part of his job was diplomacy, Gunther took a deep breath, calmed down, and replied, "in a couple of weeks."

CHAPTER 19

Cheryl's dining room table served as her office for the day. Both she and Pythia sat next to each other with their laptop computers propped open. The rest of the table was covered with trays of delicious edibles and bottles of unopened wine.

"What a horrible thing to happen to some of the drill crew!" Pythia said while reviewing the veterinary reports that scrolled on her computer screen.

Cheryl shuddered while thinking about the nine men that she occasionally socialized with. She knew their wives and children by name. Although the nine, dead men moved in different circles from the scientists'; her son, Fly, was close to the nine men since he crewed with them day in and day out. And because Fly was close to them, by association, she too had occasions to strike up conversations with them and their families.

"Quite horrible," was all she could say.

Looking up from her computer screen and locking eyes with Cheryl, Pythia said, "thanks to Fly, Otto is still with us."

A chill ran down Cheryl's spine. "Otto's recovering quickly. Fly won't leave his side."

Pythia nodded, and said, "I am happy that they have each other to talk through that tragedy."

Cheryl nodded, and said, "absolutely. I cannot get no more than two meaningful words from Fly. Whenever I ask him about anything of consequence, he clams up and broods. He was like that since he became a teenager."

Pythia smiled, shook her head, and said, "my Alicia is not like that at all. She overloads me with information. Too much information! So much so that I wish she would learn to brood. On another subject, I just love Fly's name. Is it a family name, or does it have some other meaning?"

Cheryl chuckled, and replied, "his given first name is William. However, when he became a teenager, he deemed the name, William, to be a slave name. So, he took the name: Fly. I think it is the name of a *Rap,* music video."

Pythia nodded her head, smiled, and said, "you got to admire the power of choice."

"Along those lines, I really love your name," Cheryl said. "Is *it* a family name?"

Pythia mused, then replied, "as you know, I come from generations of Mayans. That is on my mother's side.

However, my father is from Greece. He named me after the famous *Oracle of Delphi*: Pythia. She was a priestess who held court in a temple dedicated to the Greek god: Apollo."

"Oracle?" Cheryl mused.

"Yes, oracles were a gateway to the gods. Pythia was priestess to Apollo. She foretold the future. I think that my father was so impressed with the long line of shamans on my mother's side that he thought I might inherit those mystical abilities," Pythia said with a wave of her hand.

"I am duly impressed," Cheryl said.

"You don't think that stuff is *mumbo jumbo*?"

"Not at all!" Cheryl replied. "What is *mumbo jumbo* is what people call anything they do not understand, when they can't see beyond their noses. The absurdity applies when they don't acknowledge that humanity is filled with undiscovered riches."

Surprised to hear such broad thinking from an esteemed scientist, Pythia smiled contentedly.

"Red or white?" Cheryl asked while nodding at the wine selection that graced the dining room's table.

"Let's start with red," Pythia said with a smile.

"By the way, are you going to the celebration of the colony's anniversary today?" Cheryl asked after she uncorked a bottle of red wine.

"I might go for a little while. But I promised Alicia that I would help her get ready for her evening."

"Oh?" Cheryl inquired. "What is your young *Miss* doing this evening?

"Gregory invited her to Bio-1's colonial celebration."

Cheryl curiously arched her eyebrows, and asked, "are they an item?"

Pythia nodded, and said, "they've seen each other a few times."

After the women prepared their plates with appetizers and sat down with a glass of wine, they began scouring the data records.

Cheryl sipped wine while she scrolled through three years of seismic readings. "This could take forever," she said.

"Wait," Pythia said, "before you dive deeper into the seismic data, let me find the anomalous medical reports."

Pythia scrolled through the veterinary records. "Aha!" She proclaimed. "Look at your records for March of this year."

Following Pythia's suggestion, Cheryl bypassed all the previous years of identical readings and focused on the month of March. Then, spotting an abnormal, seismic reading, she said, "this is it! We had a 3.0 magnitude Mars-quake around that time. Before then the readings were between 0.0 and 1.0"

"Is a magnitude of 3.0 dangerous?"

"No, not to humans," Cheryl replied. "The more destructive quakes are from 5.0 and above. But this is more than we've had since we have been taking readings."
Energized by the correlation, Cheryl said with an eager grin, "give me another date to look up."

Pythia scrolled through her records, pointed at a report of chickens laying eggs that contained triple embryos, and said, "try the first week in April."

Cheryl eyed the computerized seismic charts, and said, "will you look at that! From March onward the readings remained at 3.0. Now, in April they shot up to 3.5."

Sighting the 3.5 reading, Pythia asked, "do you know when we started drilling for the new energy source?"

Turning her attention from the seismic readings and looking squarely at Pythia, Cheryl pondered, "I can't say for sure, but I think the drilling schedule was discussed at our February operations' meeting."

Pythia opened an additional computer screen. She found the minutes of the February operations meeting. Each month the heads of power, aquaponics, and husbandry gather to get updates on each other's operations. This meeting not only served as an information exchange, but also as a boost to comradery.

Pythia sipped from her wine glass, and said, "you are right, Cheryl. The geothermal drilling began in early March. Just from these two data points we have noticed a connection between animal behavior and seismic readings. Now, let us look at one from this month, when my larger animals were affected. Look at your data for May 12th. That's when one of our cows exhibited nausea and disorientation."

With Pythia leaning over her shoulder, Cheryl lightly scrolled down the computer screen. Although she wanted to find a connection, she was afraid. However, as soon as they approached May 12th, they saw a noticeable increase in seismic activity. "Oh my! Here is a seismic reading of 4.0," she said.

"It is not quite enough for humans to be concerned about, but our livestock surely felt it."

The two women sat in deep thought silently drinking their wine. After a few moments of pondering, Cheryl said, "I am afraid this is not good news."

Thinking about her daughter's dreams—which contained the looming threat of a violent catastrophic event—Pythia took another sip of her wine and remained silent.

Standing with her wine glass in one hand and the half-full bottle of red wine in the other, Cheryl nodded towards the living room, and said, "come on, we should get comfortable."

The two women walked to the living room, slumped into the overstuffed sofa, and filled their glasses with more wine.

After downing a sip, Pythia asked, "do you think that the seismic readings are going to increase in magnitude?"

Cheryl explained, "normally, when monitoring seismic readings, they *hum*—if you will—at a certain level. Their deviation from this *hum* is usually sharp and short-lived. However, these readings are not humming at a certain level, they are steadily increasing."

"What does that mean?"

"I don't know," Cheryl shrugged her shoulders. "Mind you, all my knowledge is based upon Earth's geologic records. And Mars is quite a different rock. However, if I had to guess, I believe that we are experiencing a buildup to a massive event."

Although alarmed, Pythia calmly asked, "do you know when this event will happen?"

Cheryl shook her head, and replied, "no I don't know. We are unable to predict earthquakes," she said solemnly.

The two women—whose husbands died just a year ago—fell silent. In silence, they both remembered their horrific losses. And, in silence, they both feared for their children's future.

After gulping more wine, Cheryl perked up, and said, "I have an idea."

Silently, Pythia rapidly nodded in encouragement.

Cheryl stood, and said, "let's go back to our laptops and make a simple line graph."

The women went to the dining room, refilled their glasses, and took a fresh plate of food. They made a line graph—one axis lay horizontal and the other axis lay vertical—in the shape of an *L*. The horizontal axis represented the *time* of the seismic readings while the vertical axis represented the seismic reading corresponding to the anomalous, animal behavior. After they had several data points plotted on their chart, the women sat back and stared at it.

"What do you see?" Pythia asked.

Feeling a little lightheaded from the already two glasses of wine, Cheryl said, "nothing. And this wine isn't helping."

Unacknowledging Cheryl's comment about the wine's effect on their science, Pythia sipped more wine, then asked, "on what scale are earthquakes measured?"

103

Still staring at the plot, Cheryl replied, "they are measured on the *Richter Scale*."

"Well," said Pythia while pointing at the graph, "our x-axis has time units in days…."

Before Pythia could finish her sentence, Cheryl perked up, and said, "Pythia, you are a genius! You are right, our y-axis should reflect the *Richer Scale* and be converted to logarithms."

Cheryl changed the y-axis to logarithms and a clear trend revealed itself. While both women stared at the graph, they emptied the remaining bottle of wine into their glasses and gulped.

CHAPTER 20

After Pythia and Cheryl packed up their laptop computers, they immediately contacted Gunther. Since Gunther had a prime table at Maria's Cantina where he watched the Colonial-Days' parade, the two women decided to meet him there.

Upon exiting Cheryl's apartment and entering the bright streets filled with happy, loud people, the two women headed for the cantina. While clutching their laptop computers, the two safely made it to Gunther's table.

Gunther stood as the two ladies approached. "Please join me," he said.

Looking at all the happy people that paraded by the outdoor seating area, Cheryl asked, "how did you get such a primo table?"

"Our sons were here first, and I just joined them about a half hour ago," he said.

After the ladies seated themselves, a waitress appeared, and asked, "may I get you ladies something to drink?"

Although slightly tipsy from the bottle of wine they shared, both women nodded.

"Red wine, please," Cheryl said.

Pythia nodded, and added, "make that two."

"So, what is so important that you two had to work on a holiday?" Gunther asked.

Before either of them answered, the waitress returned with their drinks. Then noticing that the table was already filled with appetizers, the waitress did not ask if they needed a menu.

Upon the waitress' departure, Cheryl moved her chair closer to Gunther's, whipped open her laptop computer, and said, "Pythia and I were comparing animal behavior to seismic events."

Gunther looked first at the table listing anomalous events and next at the logarithmic chart. With his keen, engineering eyes, he needed no further explanation. As he digested the information both Pythia and Cheryl gulped their wines.

"Are you sure this is correct?" Gunther asked.

Knotting her eyebrows while scratching her head, Cheryl replied, "you must understand that this analysis is based on a correlation between animal behavior and seismic readings; something that has not been peer-reviewed."

Pythia added, "you might say that it is our best guess."

Cheryl watched the masses of people streaming by them on the other side of the rope. Although it was only in the afternoon, most of the parade-goers were very much drunk. She smiled at them, and said, "Eat, drink and be merry..."

"Surely, this analysis can't be right," Gunther said.

Cheryl nodded, and said, "like Pythia said, it is our best guess."

The women looked at Gunther as he too gulped the remainder of beer from his mug. Gunther gave out a long, slow whistle, sat back in his chair, and said, "if this says what I think it does then we only have less than a week to live."

Both women sat silent.

"So, we are expecting a Mars-quake?" Gunther asked. "How large of one?"

Cheryl shook her head, and replied, "not just a Mars-quake. If you look at the graph, we are expecting an event of biblical proportions."

"Put that into scientific terms," Gunther demanded.

"The event that this graph predicts goes beyond the seismic scale. I believe that there will be a volcanic eruption," Cheryl said.

"What do you mean," Pythia asked.

"We chose this particular Martian site to colonize because of the geothermal energy beneath the surface," Cheryl began. "Our colony sits on a massive super-volcano. I think that the drilling was a catalyst that reactivated these mostly dormant volcanoes. And, the mini-Mars-quakes, that the animals were sensitive to, was due to activity in the subsurface magma chambers."

Pythia's eyes widened in understanding. "So, you mean that if there is a massive volcanic eruption, then there is no place on this planet we can escape."

Cheryl nodded.

"What do we do?" Pythia asked again.

This time, Gunther nodded, and said, "we make the beacon our priority. We send out a distress call. I will begin working on it immediately. And tomorrow morning I will get Otto and Fly to help." With those words Gunther stood up, nodded to the ladies, and headed to the power plant.

CHAPTER 21

By the time Pythia returned to her apartment, her mind was soaring from the day's events. However, upon stepping inside, she was filled with joy at the sight of her daughter. Dressed in an ivory, form-fitting gown that extended between the knee and ankle, Alicia looked like a goddess. Not only did the color of the gown contrasts nicely with her olive skin, but her hourglass figure amplified her beauty.

"Mom, you are just in time," Alicia said as she greeted Pythia with a warm hug.

Pythia held her daughter at arm's length, looked at her from head to toe, smiled, and said, "how lovely you are! My beautiful daughter."

Beaming, Alicia went to the kitchen, poured her mother a glass of wine then sat on a stool, and said, "Mom, I need you to style my hair."

A high countertop encircled the kitchen; the counter partitioned the kitchen from the living-room. On the living-room's side of the counter were three stools. Alicia had previously placed a towel on the countertop. A brush, a comb, hairspray, and hair pins laid on the towel.

Looking at the organized beauty supplements, Pythia said, "I take it you want your hair styled in an updo?"

"Yeah," Alicia replied. "If you could pull some hair up in the back and let some hair fall towards my face; that would be fine."

Pythia took a sip of wine, placed it back on the counter. A little unsteady from all the wine she had drank during the day, she decided not to drink any more until she finished Alicia's hair. After styling her daughter's hair, Pythia took a picture of the lovely girl. Knowing that they may only have a few days left to live, she hugged her daughter, kissed her on the cheek, and said, "have a great time, sweetie. And tell Gregory that I said hello."

"Don't wait up," Alicia said as she exited their apartment.

Pythia retrieved her wine, whirled the sumptuous drink about the glass, and said, "that won't be a problem."

Alone in the apartment and after drinking another glass of wine, Pythia went to her bedroom. Now, in a near-drunken state, she undressed, crawled underneath the bed covers, and drifted off to sleep. To her surprise, however, she did not slumber long.

110

Suddenly, she was awaking. She found herself in a vast, empty hall. She sat on a three-legged stool which straddled a jagged crack in the stone floor. Intoxicating vapors emanated from the crack. With both feet and shoulders bare, Pythia was dressed in a delicate, rust-colored gown that was accentuated with a long, broad, red scarf that lavishly covered her head, wrapped around one shoulder, and fell down her lap. In one hand she held an olive branch and in the other she held a bowl. While sitting on the three-legged stool, Pythia breathed in the inebriating vapors. With closed eyes, she took deep breaths.

Upon opening her eyes, she looked about massive, empty hall, and said to herself, "this must be a dream. I most certainly had too much wine." She then looked down at the translucent, rust-colored gown that she wore. The tantalizing gown was embroidered with a band of detailed needlework that encircle its hem as well as red flowers throughout. Admiringly looking at this sheer gown, Pythia was thankful that the room was not well lit. Except for discreetly placed embroidery, she appeared mostly nude. Pythia examined the delicate frock, and said, "dream or not, I love this gown."

While breathing in the vapors, Pythia saw a bright light appear at the far end of the hall. The light began to brighten. As it brightened, it lit up the darkened room. Pythia panicked when she noticed that as the light brightened, it began moving towards her.

"Deep breaths," she said to herself, "deep breaths! Remember, this is just a dream."

Although the light made her eyes water, it mesmerized her, and she continued to stare. With tears flowing down her face, she watched as the incredible brightness formed into a man. Before her, stood a tall, young man. This man was completely nude save for a silk cape draped around his neck and wrapped around an extended arm. The over six-feet-tall man had the muscular body that most gym-goers would envy. Unnervingly, Pythia recognized him instantly. With a head of golden curls, a hairless chest highlighted with bulging muscles, and eyes as clear as a blue sky; this man could only be the Greek, mythological god, Apollo. In one hand he carried his trademark, stringed instrument, a *lyre,* and in the other he carried a scroll. The god glided towards Pythia, laid the six-inch scroll in her bowl, and said with a smile, "my Pythia. You must prepare everyone for *my special day.*"

Before Pythia could say anything—ask a question—she woke up.

With a flushed face and a pounding heart, she said, "it was a dream." However, when she looked at her right hand, she was holding a six-inch, golden scroll.

CHAPTER 22

Gregory's eyes widened with delight as Alicia entered the ballroom. Never in his life had he seen someone so beautiful. Nervously, he weaved through the massive crowd of posh partygoers to meet his date.

Alicia stood as still as a statue while taking in the rich surroundings filled with equally fashionable people. She counted at least twenty, seven-layered, crystal chandeliers hanging from the ceiling. The room was so large that more than five, live, bands were stationed throughout. Music such as piano classics, jazz, and swing played softly in various corners of the room without clashing with each other.

"You look amazing!" Was all Gregory could say.

Mesmerized by her surroundings, Alicia did not notice Gregory's approach and was startled by his voice.

"Oh!" She said with a slight giggle. "This room is the heart of sophistication."

Gregory slightly bowed, locked arms with Alicia, and said, "let me show you around."

While the two bobbed and weaved throughout the crowd that was composed of a combination of Bio-1's residents and high-level supervisors from Bio-2, Alicia thought that her dream had come true. She always wanted to be with the Bio-1 crowd. But, since she did not have the talents that her friends: Otto and Fly, had; she knew she would never win a talent contest to secure a place in this splendid society. And, although she loved the community in Bio-2, she would gladly accept a chance to live in Bio-1.

After weaving through the crowd, Gregory decided to stop at the Jazz ensemble. With the background of smooth jazz filtering through the air, the two smiled at each other. Before they said a word to one another, a group of servers immediately surrounded them. As the servers glided away, Alicia and Gregory found one hand holding a glass of champagne and the other holding a bite-sized appetizer.

Alicia took a sip of the champagne and with opulent, sparkling eyes said, "so this is how the other half lives."

Both proud and embarrassed at the same time, Gregory nodded. However, before he could utter a word, they were joined by a strikingly tall man with a thick head of hair and an equally thick mustache.

"Gregory, please introduce me to this lovely lady," the man said.

Gregory was both annoyed and surprised by the interruption. "Alicia, I would like you to meet my father, Boris Andreevich."

Alicia knew of Boris Andreevich. Everyone in the colony knew of Boris Andreevich. He was the force behind the Martian colonization. Everyone knew the story about how he brokered a deal between the riches men on Earth to pool their resources and create the technology needed to colonize Mars.

Although she knew that she was in the presence of royalty, Alicia was determined not to let her nerves show. So, she steadfastly locked eyes with Boris, extended her hand for a handshake, and said, "pleased to meet you, Mr. Andreevich."

Boris took Alicia's outstretched hand, turned it palm-side down, and graced it with a tender kiss.

"Please call me Boris," he charmingly said. Then straightening up, but not letting go of her hand, he asked, "are you the daughter of the veterinarian?"

Surprised that he knew such a minor detail, Alicia smiled, and replied, "yes, I am."

Gregory cleared his throat, and boasted, "Alicia is managing the aquaponics plant."

Uncomfortable moments passed as Boris sized up Alicia. However, before the awkward conversation continued, Heather joined the threesome.

Turning his attention to Heather, Boris' eyes lit up. Looking at the lovely, young teen wearing a pink, princess gown; Boris became entranced. Centuries of tradition was ingrained in Boris. Tradition that defined Heather as the picture of beauty. Men, like Boris, sought after girls like Heather. Fair-skinned girls with large, blue eyes and waist-length, blond curls were highly prized. And, although Boris was intrigued by Alicia's exotic features, he would much prefer that his son mate with someone closer to a classic European beauty like Heather.

Heather immediately locked arms with Gregory; then after acknowledging Alicia with a nod and a smile, she alluringly batted her eyelashes at Boris, and asked, "do you mind if I steal your son away for a few minutes? I have something to show him."

Pleased to see them together, Boris replied, "not at all. I can keep Miss Alicia company until you return."

Alicia's panic-stricken eyes widened.

Not wanting to leave Alicia alone with his father, Gregory said, "I am busy now, Heather. I can catch up with you later."

Heather was not taking *no* for an answer. She lightly tugged on Gregory's arm, and said, "we will be gone only a few minutes. Please," she begged.

Alicia took a deep breath, and said, "don't worry about me. I will be okay. Just don't be too long."

After Gregory and Heather departed, Boris asked Alicia, "who is your sponsor?"

Alicia knew of the six riches men that pooled their funds to colonize Mars. These men, from various countries around the world, recruited people from their locations for the colony. She also knew that both her mother and father were recruited by a Venezuelan oil-baron who had sordid ties with the Mexican Drug Cartel.

"Señor Carlos Ortega," Alicia replied.

"Ahh, Carlos," Boris said with a fond smile, "a smart man. Did either of your parents work for him?"

Alicia nodded, and replied, "my father was a top scientist in Senor Ortega's oil business. My father was a geophysicist."

Upon hearing Alicia speak of her father in the past tense, Boris suddenly realized that Alicia's father was amongst the scientists who died along with his son. However, before he offered sympathy, they were joined by George Andrews: Bio-1's top surgeon.

Upon nearing the piano band where they were out of earshot of Boris, Gregory asked, "what can be so important?"

Noticing how Gregory finished the glass of champagne, Heather grabbed two additional glasses from a passing waiter, handed one to Gregory, and said, "you are going to need more of this once I tell you what I discovered."

Annoyed with Heather, Gregory asked, "what did you discover?"

"Remember when Fly and Otto were talking about winning the talent contest?"

Gregory nodded.

"So that they could win either residency in Bio-1 or a trip back to Earth?"

Annoyed, Gregory answered, "yes. So?"

"Well, I looked into the last three winners."

117

"And?" Gregory impatiently asked.

Heather squirmed, and replied, "they didn't go back to Earth."

Knowing that all the spaceships used to transport the colony to Mars were scrapped to complete the habitats, Gregory shrugged his shoulders, and said, "then they must be living in Bio-1."

Heather slowly shook her head. "No. They don't reside here either."

"Where else can they be? Fly said that every person who won the talent contest went to Bio-1 or Earth."

Heather bowed her head. After a moment of silence, she guiltily looked into Gregory's eyes, and said, "they are all dead."

As a soft piano sonata played in the background, a chill ran down Gregory's spine.

"What? How can they be dead? Why?"

Heather directed Gregory's attention to her uncle, Clive, who stood taking to two others just a few feet away from them.

"When we were having the drilling-accident debriefing at the power plant, I noticed my uncle's eyes."

Gregory shook his head, and asked, "what are you talking about?"

"His eyes used to be a light brown and tired looking. Now, they are bright blue and youthful."

"So?" Gregory said.

In answer to Gregory's question, Heather redirected his attention to another man standing a few feet away from them. The tall, blustering man heartily laughed as he drank a glass of vodka.

"And look at your uncle over there. Didn't he have health issues for months? Was it his liver? Didn't he need a transplant?"

Gregory noticed his uncle, Michael, who drank vodka with gusto. He recalled that his uncle's health was deteriorating to the point that they were making funeral plans.

While the music played and Gregory remained silent, Heather explained, "I found out that every contestant must receive a complete physical before they can compete. And even though the audience can vote to choose the winner, our votes do not count. The winner is chosen by which of Bio-1's privileged needs a body part."

Stunned, Gregory remained silent.

"So, whoever wins," Heather continued, "is stripped of their organs which are then distributed amongst the powerful people in Bio-1. And, in some cases, these people are not even sick. They just want to prolong their lives."

After a few moments of silence, Gregory spouted, "that can't be right. That is barbaric! Are you sure?"

Heather nodded, and said, "after I figured this out, I knew that I needed proof. So, I checked dates, times, illnesses, and hospital records. These data all agree with my conclusions."

Gregory shook his head in disgust, and asked rhetorically, "why am I not surprised?" He then looked at his uncle who was previously bedridden and expected to get worse. "What a bastard," he said about his uncle.

Heather, who normally cared only about herself, now showed empathy for others. Even though this empathy grew out of her own interest in Fly—and not wanting him to die—it suddenly blossomed with the understanding that people her age were being killed for their body parts.

Gregory looked across the room at his father and Alicia who were joined by Bio-1's top surgeon. As this unholy news sunk in, he turned and headed towards Alicia. However, before he took a step in their direction, Heather grabbed his arm, and said, "we have to somehow discourage Fly and Otto from entering the talent contest."

Gregory nodded in agreement. He turned away from Heather and raced towards Alicia.

Once at Alicia's side, Gregory took her hand, nodded towards the entrance, and said, "we have to go."

"But" Alicia said while apologetically looking at the men she was engaged with.

Gregory all but yanked Alicia away from his father leaving the two men with surprised looks on their faces.

Upon exiting the main hall, Alicia asked, "have I done something wrong?"

Gregory shook his head and silently led her to the river where he slumped on a picnic bench.

In the short time she knew Gregory, Alicia had never seen him so distraught. "What's wrong?" She asked.

Gregory felt hot. His face was flushed red. Although ashamed of this news, he looked pleading into Alicia's eyes, and explained Heather's findings.

After hearing the ghastly account, Alicia slumped on the picnic bench next to Gregory.

"Those monsters!" She yelled.

Silently, Gregory looked at the bright stars above the domed ceiling. Since Mars had less of an atmosphere than Earth's, the stars were brilliant. He often found himself lying on the grass next to the river at night after his brother's death. He would silently look to the brilliant stars for a meaning; but none came. However, after Heather's startling revelation about organ harvesting, Gregory had an epiphany. He reasoned that his brother and the scientists were killed because they knew too much. They knew that Earth was destroyed. They knew that all their spaceships' parts were incorporated in the colony's building. And, because his brother and the five scientists understood those two things, it would not be long until they understood the covert, organ-harvesting plan. Therefore, to preserve their way of life, the *New Guard* had to eliminate the threat. And elimination translated to killing everyone—even one of their own.

Although this epiphany left Gregory more devastated than before—knowing that his father was responsible for killing his own son—he forced himself to focus on his future. Taking his eyes from the stars and holding Alicia by the

121

shoulders forcing the distraught woman to look at him, he said, "tomorrow after my meeting in Bio-2, we should get together and make a plan."

Alicia stared into his pleading eyes, and asked, "a plan? What can we do? Those people are powerful. They make the laws."

Seeing that Alicia's eyes were tearing, Gregory placed a gentle kiss on her lips, wiped a tear from her cheek, and said, "let us get you home. We can outsmart them. Trust me."

CHAPTER 23

"I called this meeting to update everyone on an analysis that Pythia and I conducted," Cheryl said as she looked around the table. Like their last, secret meeting, all were in attendance. Besides herself and Pythia, both Gunther and Gregory were present.

"You should all have the graph that I previously texted to your computerized pads," she continued. Cheryl paused a few moments while everyone looked at their 5-by-8-inch computer pads. She gave them a few moments to examine the graph.

"What you are looking at is a logarithmic graph. On the x-axis is time, in days, and on the y-axis are seismic readings."

"May I add something?" Pythia asked.

Cheryl nodded at her friend, and answered, "please do."

"Each seismic reading located on the y-axis corresponds to unusual animal behavior. So, these points weren't picked randomly."

Looking at the graph, Gregory scratched his head, and asked, "shouldn't seismic readings fluctuate? I mean should they reach a peak while recording a seismic event then return to a baseline reading?"

Cheryl noted that Gregory's thought processes were akin to a mature scientist.

She nodded, and replied, "you are absolutely right, Gregory."

"Then, if that is true," interrupted Gunther, "why does this graph show a steady and constant increase?"

All eyes were on Cheryl as she sighed.

"Like I mentioned before, we have little scientific data on Mars' subsurface geology."

"So, you don't know what this means?" Gunther challenged.

"What I know is, if this were a graph of Earth's subsurface, then we would be in big trouble."

"Trouble? What sort of trouble?" Gregory asked.

"Big trouble. The tremors that our livestock have been experiencing are simply a precursor to a much larger event."

Gunther nodded, and asked, "how large?"

Cheryl took a deep breath. She now decided to get to the point. "Normally, as Gregory said, seismic readings are supposed to fluctuate; or reach peaks and valleys. These readings are continuing to rise. What this tells me is there is a large magma chamber moving beneath Olympus Mons and the other three volcanoes. The pressure in this chamber is increasing."

With those words, the group fell silent. Then Gunther asked, "was the drilling accident connected to this increase in subsurface pressure?"

As Gunther's question sunk in, Cheryl nodded, and answered, "possibly."

Gunther's eyes widened. Knowing that the bio-domes could not withstand the chemical that disintegrated the drill crew's environmental suits, he saw extinction-level trouble on the horizon.

"So, this increase in pressure," Pythia began, "what exactly does that mean?"

"I believe the Tharsis Bulge is a super-volcano. And that Olympus Mons and the other volcanoes are just the tips of the proverbial iceberg. Meaning, that there would be a much larger eruption than if one of the individual volcanos erupted. So, if the pressure is increasing, the entire Tharsis Bulge will erupt." She silently bowed her head avoiding looking at Gregory. How can she tell a child that he has only days to live?

Gunther absorbed everything that Cheryl said. He knew that her conclusions were scientifically correct. However, due to his engineering way of thinking, he knew he could fix it. He could always fix things.

"If this analysis is correct, then our only hope is the beacon we created to signal the South Dakota colony; wherever they are," Gunther said.

"How is that coming along?" Gregory asked.

"Yesterday, with the help of Otto and Fly, we completed the beacon. It is sending out *SOS* distress calls as we speak."

"What if they don't reach us in time?" Gregory asked. "Can we shelter in place if the volcano erupts?"

Cheryl shook her head while she tapped her fingers on the table, and said, "I am sorry, but there is no place to hide from such a catastrophic event."

Gregory's eyes blinked in rapid succession while he thought about the bunkers in Bio-1.

"Bio-1 has underground bunkers that were designed as lifeboats just in case the domes were breached. I know they are designed for a few people, but we could cram others in them."

Gunther knew of these bunkers. They were designed only for the rich inhabitants. If the bio-domes breached, everyone else were to report to the high-bay area in Bio-3.

Gunther shook his head, and said, "no. We cannot cram the entire Martian colony into those bunkers. They were meant solely to protect a small group of Bio-1 residents. And, with the catastrophe that Cheryl is predicting, those bunkers will not survive. They may crack due to the shifting of Mars' subsurface. And if that does not destroy the bunkers, a volcanic event of that magnitude would spew out so much ash, lava, and rock that they will be buried under up to a kilometer. Besides, we don't even know when this event will happen."

"What is today's date," Pythia asked in a soft, gentle voice.

Gunther looked at his watch, and said, "today's date is June 6th."

"It will happen tomorrow. It will happen on *Apollo's Day*," Pythia said with a sigh.

CHAPTER 24

"Tomorrow!" Cheryl exclaimed. "Are you saying that the super-volcano will erupt tomorrow?"

Pythia nodded.

Once again, everyone grew silent.

Gregory was the first to break the silence, and asked, "how do you know that? How do you know that the volcano will erupt tomorrow?"

Pythia swallowed hard, looked around the table, and replied, "because tomorrow is *Apollo's Day.*"

Knowing that Pythia was named after the Oracle of Delphi—the high priestess to the Greek god, Apollo—Cheryl sat back in her seat and silently waited for an explanation.

"I am trained in classic Greek history," Gregory said. "And I do know that the seventh day of the month is the day set aside for the Greek god, Apollo. But what does that have to do with tomorrow?"

Although Pythia believed her vision, she was not sure if anyone else would. She took a deep breath, and said, "last night, I had a vision of Apollo. In this vision, I was dressed as my namesake, Pythia. She was his high priestess. For those of you who do not know, Pythia was the Oracle of Delphi during the time when the Greek gods reigned. And, through Pythia, Apollo delivered his prophecies. Well, last night he spoke to me."

Gunther laughed, shook his head, and belted, "nonsense! You must admit that yesterday was *Colonial Day*, and everyone had an alcoholic drink or two. Hell, you had one with Cheryl and I yesterday. You mustn't mistake alcoholic delusions for absolute truths."

"You shouldn't be so dismissive," Gregory said to Gunther. "Several of us are having lucid dreams. I have had one. My dream—like some dreams that others had—is of a bright, new world. It was a dream of hope for a bright future."

Cheryl saw that Gunther was ready for a fight. She knew that he dealt in facts and numbers; as did she. However, she also knew that truths were more than facts and numbers. She put a hand on Gunther's, and said, "Pythia's anecdotal evidence made our graph possible. Because of animal senses, we were able to figure out that there is an event coming. Let us hear what she has to say."

129

Pythia looked around the table, and said, "Apollo told me to remember his day and to prepare. Then he gave me a scroll."

"A scroll?" Gunther asked. "Did you read it before you woke up from that fantastical dream?"

Pythia impatiently leveled Gunther a searing glare, and replied, "no. I couldn't read it because it was written in the Greek language."

Gunther thrusts his hands into the air, and proclaimed, "this is ridiculous!"

Gregory leaned on the table while locking eyes with Pythia, and said, "I know the Greek language. Can you remember any of the characters written on the scroll?"

Pythia smiled, reached into her satchel, pulled out an object, handed it to Gregory, and said, "this is the scroll that Apollo gave me. Perhaps, you can decipher its meaning."

Upon seeing this scroll, the group was aghast. Not one of them had ever known of physical objects transferring from visions or dreams!

Hesitantly, Gregory took the object. It was composed of two, six-inch, golden cylinders that were attached to a delicate paper.

He carefully laid the scroll on the table and sheepishly looked at Pythia for permission to unroll it.

Pythia nodded.

Everyone stood from their chairs to get a better view of the object as Gregory laid it open.

Gregory tried not to breathe on the paper. In a hushed voice, he asked, "what type of paper do you think this is?"

"I think the paper is made of papyrus," Pythia answered. "And" she said while gently touching one of the cylinders, "I think these are made of pure gold."

When the scroll was opened to its fullest extent, one word appeared on the papyrus: προετοιμάζω.

"Can you read that?" Pythia asked Gregory.

"Yes. I can," Gregory replied. "You know that both the Greek and Russian languages are loosely based upon the *Cyrillic* alphabet. Because of that, Greek was an easy language for me to learn when I was a child."

"Well?" Asked Gunther. "What does that word mean?"

Gregory looked each one in the eyes, then said, "it means: *prepare*."

"Prepare," Pythia whispered as she allowed the word to roll off her tongue.

"Prepare for what?" Gunther asked.

Silently, everyone sat down in their seats and stared at the opened scroll. They all had so many questions. Cheryl wondered how a solid object could materialize from a dream. Gunther questioned his sanity for entertaining such non-scientific thoughts. And, Pythia who knew that the original Pythia's predictions were vague, at best, questioned why Apollo gave her a precise prediction.

131

Pythia smiled, then said, "we must prepare for tomorrow. Given this information; if the super-volcano erupts tomorrow, then we must get everyone ready."

This all made sense to Gregory. He took Pythia at her word. He now realized that they will be rescued. That all the dreams and now the warning was building up to this moment of clarity.

Gunther vigorously shook his head, and said, "this is crazy. I am going back to work."

Cheryl locked eyes with Gunther. Her searing stare froze him.

"Listen Gunther, we cannot prepare without you. Whether you believe in Pythia's message or not, we need you to help us; to help us all."

Gunther sighed, and asked, "what can we do? How can we prepare?"

"First," said Cheryl, "we need a reason for everyone to take off work tomorrow. We need to gather them into the high-bay area."

Gregory looked puzzled, and asked, "Why?"

"If we assume that we are going to be rescued," Cheryl began, "then we need everyone in one area. I believe that this volcano will awaken with an explosion. That blast will leave us little time to gather people."

Even though Gunther put little faith in visions and dreams, he respected Cheryl. He knew that she was world renowned for her scientific exploits. So, he decided to put his faith in her.

132

Gunther hopelessly threw his hands into the air, and said, "I can do that. After we leave this meeting, I will inform the managers that we discovered minor structural weaknesses in Bios 1 and 2. And, since these repairs could likely lead to a major weakness—possibly loss of environmental containment—we must require that everyone from Bios 1 and 2 gather in Bio-3's high-bay area."

Gregory nodded in agreement, and said, "that is a brilliant ploy!"

Pythia perked up, and added, "after Gunther makes the announcement, I will text folks to bring food and drink. Why not make it a party?"

Gunther laughed, and said, "eat, drink, and be merry for tomorrow we die."

Cheryl smiled, nudged Gunther with an elbow, and said, "for tomorrow we live!"

CHAPTER 25

Early the next morning, Gunther instructed his work-crew to clear out the high-bay area of everything. Even though there was equipment such as drilling vehicles, powerplant generators, batteries, ladders, and the like; it took less than two hours to complete. While the work-crew were clearing out these major pieces of equipment, Cheryl and Pythia were busy making the extremely spacious warehouse welcoming to the incoming crowd.

Pythia gathered others, including Alicia and Gregory, to help setup tables, chairs, and bars. Cheryl not only coordinated with every restaurant for them to setup satellite cafés, but she also put both Fly and Otto in charge of entertainment. By midday, the high-bay area was transformed from an equipment storage and staging area to a country fair complete with food, music, and masses of people.

Standing with Gunther at her side, Cheryl looked at the happy colonists, and asked, "do you think they have a clue of what is going to happen?"

Gunther sighed and replied, "no, I doubt they would have a clue. If *anything* happens."

Pythia now joined the two, and asked, "do you two think it is getting hot in here?"

Gunther nodded, and said, "when you put almost two-thousand people in an enclosed area, heat builds up."

Pythia shook her head, and said, "I know that. I mean that there is more than body heat in here. We know that our heating and cooling systems can automatically accommodate massive amounts of people in one area. We've had events like this before."

Gunther, who also knew this, said, "I will go to the power-plant's control-room and examine the settings."

Standing next to Pythia, Cheryl was silent. Silently, she watched as her Martian neighbors went from booth to booth gathering food and drink. Silently, she watched as people enjoyed the clear tones that Fly and Otto rapped. And, silently, she thought of the massive lake of magma beneath them churning its way up to the Martian surface.

Pythia noticed that Cheryl was smiling with tears falling from her eyes. She knew that Cheryl was worried about the coming event. However, she was certain that they were to be rescued. She grabbed her friend's hand, looked her in the eyes, and said, "I know that you are worried, but I promise you that we will be okay."

Pythia gently touched Cheryl's face and dried her tears. Cheryl looked at her friend and colleague. She not only saw tenderness in Pythia's face, but she also saw hope. Knowing that she too had to be hopeful, if not for herself, but for everyone else—including Fly—she repeatedly nodded, sucked in a deep breath, and said, "if not for you, Pythia, I would have given up long ago. I have faith in you. And, if you say that we will be okay, then I believe it."

Gunther returned and stood alongside Pythia and Cheryl.

"The increase in temperature is more than body heat," Gunther reported.

Cheryl worriedly looked at her two friends, and said, "I fear that the magma chamber is not only getting full, but it is surfacing. Do we have all of the colonists here?"

"Everyone is accounted for except the six colonial managers and their families," Gunther replied.

"Why aren't they here?" Pythia asked.

"Each manager has his own underground bunker. When I briefed them on the structural situation, they decided to retreat to their bunkers," Gunther replied.

Cheryl looked around the high-bay area and noticed that both Gregory and Heather were present.

Gunther noticed the direction of her search and in anticipation to her question, he said, "even though Gregory managed to roundup the majority of Bio-1's inhabitants, both his and Heather's families decided to ride out any possible structural mishaps in their luxurious bunkers."

136

Cheryl was slightly annoyed that Gunther anticipated her question. However, she put her annoyance aside when she felt a slight tremor beneath her feet, and said, "did you guys feel that?"

Both Pythia and Gunther slowly nodded.

"Thankfully, with all of the music, eating, and drinking; no one else felt it," Cheryl said.

When the quakes strengthened, Gunther wanted to avoid a mass panic. Seeing nearly two-thousand people crammed in an enclosed space, he envisioned a stampede of frightened individuals. He, therefore, took a slow, deep breath, and said, "I am going to make an announcement."

With wide eyes, Cheryl asked, "an announcement? About what?"

"We don't want a panic. If you are right, these tremors are going to increase. And, the last thing we need in this enclosed area, is people running and trampling each other."

"What are you going to tell them?" Pythia wanted to know.

"The truth," he said then headed to the raised platform where Otto and Fly were preforming.

Both Cheryl and Pythia followed Gunther to the raised platform. Seeing their parents climb on stage, Otto and Fly stopped rapping.

"I need to make an announcement," Gunther said to the two, young men.

After Fly and Otto stepped aside, Gunther took the microphone, and said, "ladies and gentlemen I have something to tell you."

With those words, the entire high-bay area went silent. Everyone knew Gunther. They knew that he was the last remaining engineer who made the Martian colony possible. They knew that through his leadership they were safe. They knew that he was a man of very few words. Consequently, they knew that when he spoke, they needed to listen.

Before continuing to speak, Gunther looked at his son, Otto, and gave him a gentle smile.

"What we told you previously about the structural defects in the bio-domes was a ruse," he began. "It was a ruse to get all of you together in one location." He paused and beckoned both Pythia and Cheryl to his side. Then looking down at the crowd, he spotted Gregory. He nodded to Gregory, and said, "Gregory would you please join us on the stage."

While Gregory wound his way to the stage, murmurs rose from the crowd.

After Pythia, Cheryl, Gregory, and Gunther occupied the front of the stage centering on the microphone, Fly—who stood on the back part of the stage with Otto—said to his friend, "do you know what this is all about?"

Otto shook his head and replied, "your guess is as good as mine."

With Gunther flanked by his cohorts, he continued and said, "during the past few days, we were conducting a somewhat scientific investigation into several incidents. As you all know we had a tragic drilling accident where several of our community were either injured or died. And, that accident was only part of other incidents such as animal behavior and anomalous seismic readings. Through our investigation, we found out that there is going to be a volcanic eruption here on Mars."

With those words, all the murmurs subsided, and silence gripped the crowd.

After a few seconds of silence someone in the crowd yelled, "eruption!"

Following that exclamation, someone else screamed, "if those massive volcanos erupt, we will surely die!"

Gunther nodded in agreement, held up his hands, and said, "if we stay here on Mars, we will die."

With those words, some of the crowd screamed in terror while others began to cry. Seeing that Gunther's words had the opposite effect on the crowd than was intended, Cheryl nudged him away from the microphone and began to speak to the crowd. "Calm down everyone," she said. "Gunther is right. If we stay on Mars, we will die. However, there is a group of Earthlings who are on their way to rescue us."

"It took several trips for us to get here from Earth," another person yelled from the crowd. "How can we all be rescued at once?"

Pythia took the microphone from Cheryl. As she did, Gunther bowed his head and whispered to Cheryl, "I don't think they will believe her *mumbo jumbo*."

139

"Gregory, will you tell everyone about the South Dakota colonists?" Pythia asked and handed Gregory the microphone.

Gregory looked over the crowd of approximately two-thousand people, and said, "several years ago, a colony from South Dakota—a colony about as large as ours—departed Earth in one, massive spaceship and traveled to the stars. Knowing that our brothers and sisters are still out in space, we constructed a beacon to contact them."

"Did we get in touch with them? Did they reply?" Another frantic voice asked.

Gregory, now perspiring profusely from the increased heat, noticed that not only was everyone on stage sweating, but the entire crowd was becoming sweat-drenched and lethargic. After looking over the anxious, though sluggish, crowd, Gregory knew that he had to calm them. His only recourse was to lie. So, he answered, "yes. They contacted us back and said they would be here today."

Before anyone said another word, a tremor struck. This time the tremor was more of a stronger quake. The quake shook the high-bay area causing tables and chairs to tumble and people to crumble. Although the quake was somewhat alarming, the crowd was becoming even more exhausted from the heat and, therefore, did not react to the jolt.

Cheryl took the microphone. She decided she needed to say something to soothe the crowd. However, before she said anything, the large, garage-like door, located at the back of the hangar, began to open.

140

Even though everyone knew that after those doors opened, they would be exposed to Mars' toxic atmosphere—they were too hot and lethargic to panic. So, everyone braced themselves as the door opened.

But, instead of toxic carbon dioxide racing in and stealing their oxygen; a bright light appeared accompanied by a cool, oxygen-rich breeze. Everyone watched as a figure emerged from the light. When Pythia saw who walked towards them, she took the microphone, bowed her head, and said, "Lord Apollo."

Dressed in khakis and a blue t-shirt, the over six-foot tall Greek god with a mass of curly blond hair cascading around his shoulders, strolled to the stage, and embraced Pythia. After a long embrace, Apollo held Pythia at arm's length, and said, "Pythia, Pythia, Pythia—it is so good to see you again!"

Seeing Pythia's vision come to life, Gunther, Cheryl, and Gregory were aghast. However, before they said anything, Apollo took the microphone from Pythia. Then with the confidence of a god, he looked over the crowd, smiled, and announced, "my good people, I want you to walk toward the light. You must go quickly. There are others waiting for you there to help you to safety."

Silently, everyone turned towards the light and noticed other figures waiting for them. Everyone was frozen. They did not know what was happening. However, when a stronger quake struck, they perked up and ambled toward the light.

Gunther approached Apollo, hesitantly retrieved the microphone, and said, "Everyone, listen to *his* words. Go quickly towards the light!"

CHAPTER 26

Somewhat hesitantly, however quickly, everyone walked towards the bright light. Some walked by themselves while others shakenly held onto family members. As they neared the light, they saw welcoming figures beckoning them onward. Hand in hand, Alicia and Gregory entered the bright area. They were initially blinded by the brilliant light. However, as their eyes adjusted, they found themselves in a long, wide hallway. While they walked down the hallway, they were soothed by a soft piano sonata.

Holding on to one another, Alicia and Gregory walked down the hallway for ten minutes. The long hallway opened to an immense, forested area. This one mile in diameter area contained trees, waterways, and several picnic benches. This forested area, reminiscent of Bio-1's greenspace, was capped

143

with a clear transparent cover that stretched from horizon to horizon.

Cheryl, along with most of the leadership team, was the last to enter the forested area. As Cheryl entered the domed park, she immediately stationed herself near a window. When she looked through the window, she gasped at the view outside. She saw that they were hovering about one hundred feet above the Martian surface. Observing that they were still ascending towards the stars, Cheryl concluded that they were on a spaceship. However, before she tried to imagine how big a spaceship must be to have this large park, she looked down towards the Martian surface and watched the catastrophic event unfold. Not only was Cheryl glued to the window, but also was everyone else from the Martian colony.

Everyone's eyes were on the four, smoking volcanoes below. Like most volcanoes on Earth, signs of life from Olympus Mons began with puffs of smoke seeping from its cone. And like a symphony of wonder, these puffs of smoke began escaping the other volcanoes. However, unlike *modern* Earth volcanoes, vents of smoke opened near the four volcanoes and as far as two-hundred miles away. From a distance, Olympus Mons and its sister volcanoes looked like the venting slits cut in an apple pie's crust—where the four volcanoes occupied the middle of the pie crust and the over ten other smoking vents represented random slits in the crust.

Minutes following the venting, the 15-mile-high Olympus Mons violently erupted in a megaton explosion cutting its height in half. From her viewpoint, Cheryl initially saw enormous clouds of black smoke and searing rock burst from all the volcanoes. Within seconds, the volcanoes combined and formed one large eruption. The powerful, initial eruption of dark clouds contained violent streaks of lightening dancing throughout the plume. Pyroclastic flows, composed of pumice and ash, shot out during the explosion. Like water surging from a ruptured dam, pyroclastic flows raced at horrific speeds of over fifty-miles per hour and instantly obliterated the bio-domes.

Destruction of the bio-domes was not limited to its surface area. Anyone who took refuge in the subsurface bunkers were doomed. The massive amounts of ash and pumice that spew from the four volcanoes before they collapsed, added three miles of additional layering to the planet's surface. Moreover, after Olympus Mons and the other three volcanoes exploded and collapsed, the outfall debris from their shattered cones layered the ground with another mile of rocks. Consequently, anyone who survived the catastrophe in their bunkers were now buried under four miles of debris.

After the volcanic cones were obliterated, an angry ocean of lava emerged from the depths of the caldera. Like a stormy ocean, the lava churned and twisted with wave after wave breaking over each other. Red, fiery waves capped with streaks of black semi-cooled crust forcefully crashed into each other while rising to the surface. Churning like bubbles in a boiling pot, these waves were just the tip of the massive magma chamber below.

145

Lava poured with lightning speed from the caldera. Moreover, the spewing of gases, rocks, and lava continued until the massive super-volcano, formally known as the Tharsis Bulge, collapsed deeper into itself.

With the collapse of the magma chamber, the face of Mars completely changed. It no longer had a pot-belly bulge near its equator. The planet's shape became oval. And, where the super-volcano collapsed into itself; a large bowl-shaped depression remained. Furthermore, before the collapse, vents of ash and gases spewed into Mars' atmosphere creating a genesis, a new beginning. Cheryl knew that because of the gases that were dispersing in the Martian atmosphere—in thousands of years—Mars would terraform. She imagined an earth-like atmosphere and an ocean in place of the bowl-like depression left by the collapse of the super-volcano.

"You are so right," said Apollo who was now at Cheryl's side.

Startled, Cheryl looked up into this Greek god's eyes.

"I didn't say anything," she said shakily. Being in the presence of a god, weakened her knees.

Apollo slipped an arm around Cheryl's waist to steady her. He charmingly smiled, and said, "I seem to have this effect on Earthlings. Let me help you."

Feeling faint while standing next to Apollo, Cheryl took deep breaths and avoided looking at him. She focused her attention to the changing face of Mars, and asked, "what am I right about?"

Also looking at the red planet as they ascended into Space, Apollo replied, "Mars is going through terraforming. In a few thousand years it will be just like your home-world, Earth. Where the Tharsis Bulge collapsed, there will be a liquid ocean. The atmosphere will change from mostly carbon dioxide to mostly oxygen."

Realizing that he had read her mind, Cheryl trembled, and asked, "how do you know this?"

Apollo ran his free hand through his head of thick, blond hair, and simply replied, "I know this because I am Apollo the god of light and prophesy."

Part II

Life in Space

CHAPTER 1

Some unknown emotion pricked Apollo's aura as he
looked into Cheryl's eyes. Was it the fear and confusion he
sensed from her? No. It was not that. Was it her beauty? Was
it how close they were standing next to each other? No. Not
any of those either. As a god, Apollo had been sexually active
with many beautiful women—most, more beautiful than
Cheryl—and they typically stirred his sexual nature.
Something more than that. As he stood next to Cheryl while
watching Mars transform, he delighted in *not* knowing why she
intrigued him.

After the spaceship began traveling away from Mars
and towards the solar system's asteroid-belt, Apollo said,
"Doctor Greyson, we are needed in the conference room. I will
take you there."

Cheryl's eyes widened. She did not know this strange man—rather—god. Frankly, she was afraid of him. And the thought of leaving the safety of the forest—where the entire Martian colony was—frightened her even more.

As she opened her mouth to talk, Pythia appeared at Apollo's side, and said, "our hosts want us to meet in the conference room. They realized that most of us are in shock at the destruction of our home," she said to Cheryl. "They don't want to cause more harm to us by keeping us in the dark about who they are. So, they want us—me, you, Gunther, Fly, Otto, Alicia, Heather, and Gregory—to join them while they make their announcement. The others are on their way there."

Still somewhat paralyzed by the recent events, Cheryl took a deep breath and shakily clasped Pythia's hand in hers just like a non-swimmer desperately holds on to the edge of a swimming pool while immersed in its cold, deep water.

Noticing her friend's unsteadiness, Pythia warmly gripped Cheryl's hand. Then looking up into the clear, blue eyes of Apollo that were filled with questions, Pythia asked, "my lord, would you lead us to the conference room?"

With a slight nod of his head and a playful smile on his lips, Apollo led the two women out of the forested area and back into the bright, wide hallway. And, without an explanation as to where on the ship they were headed or how they were getting there, Apollo led the two ladies into what appeared to be an elevator where they exited onto another wide hallway.

As the three walked down the long hallway, Pythia froze in her steps. Cheryl also noticed how Pythia's hand gripped hers tighter than before. Next, she noticed that Pythia began to tremble. And finally, she saw Pythia drop to her knees and bow her head.

Then looking ahead, she saw a woman approaching them. The dark-brown-skinned woman in her mid-twenties was carrying a curiously looking toddler on her hip. When they were within a foot of each other, the woman handed the child to Apollo, put a free hand under Pythia's chin, and said, "please stand. There will be no bowing on this spaceship."

Shakily, Pythia stood but kept her eyes looking downward, and pronounced, "Thia, goddess of all gods, you honor me."

Cheryl's eyes widened when hearing the title Pythia bestowed on this gentle, yet unassuming woman who stood before them.

Now seeing that the two women, who he escorted to the meeting, were both trembling with anxiety and fear; Apollo broke into one of his signatures, boyish smiles, and said, "my sister, Thia, has that god-fearing effect on most people when they first meet her. However, in time, you will be amazed how gentle she can be."

Before either Pythia or Cheryl said a word, the toddler squirmed his way from Apollo's arms and hopped to the floor. Then in a typical, unsteady toddler's run he waddled towards five teenagers who approached the group. When the toddler stopped in front of Fly and held his arms up to be carried, both

151

Gregory and Alicia simultaneously gasped in disbelief. They both knew that this was the strange child from their dreams; the child that gave them hope.

Fly picked the child up, held him gently in his arms, and said, "hello little guy. What's your name?"

Thia approached the teens with a disarming smile, and said, "this is my son, Fritzie. And by the looks of it, he has a new friend."

Fly nodded while smiling at Fritzie.

"Follow me everyone," said Apollo.

The group followed Apollo into a large conference room which was already occupied with twenty others. Ten people were seated around a large table and others occupied chairs that were butted up against the room's walls.

Thia sat at the head of the table and beckoned the group to fill in the remaining, empty chairs. While Apollo sat next to Thia; Gregory, Otto, Alicia, Heather, and Fly sat next to each other.

The conference room was fully outfitted with communication devices. Imbedded in the table were computer screens associated with each seat. Also, an enormous screen wrapped around the entire room. This screen occupied space from above the chairs to the ceiling. The entire ship's complement, whether they were in the vast, forested area or located in the engine room, Bridge, or recreation halls, were displayed on this view screen. And, conversely, people in different locations had visuals of everyone in the conference room.

152

"Hello every," Thia began. "First, I would like to welcome the Martian colonists to our spaceship. And, more importantly, I want to welcome you all to our family. Some of you may know that most of us also originated from Earth. Although our community is known as the South Dakota colony, members are from all over the Earth. And second, you have my deepest sympathies for those we could not rescue," Thia said looking directly at both Heather and Gregory.

Gregory bowed his head. He knew that his father and others in Bio-1—who had built-in bunkers and did not leave—were now covered in miles of ash, rock, and lava. He knew if they survived the initial volcanic eruption, and subsequent lava flows, that their bunkers had, at most, two months of breathable air and food. Furthermore, he knew that they were doomed.

Thia broadened her gaze from Gregory and Heather. She expanded her view to everyone around the room, and continued, "you are now part of our family. I know you must have many questions about who we are and where we are taking you. After this meeting adjourns, several of our people will gather you all into groups and give you a tour of this spaceship and, subsequently, assign you to living quarters."

Gunther, who was already seated in the conference room when the others joined them, raised his hand. When Thia acknowledged him with a slight nod of her head, he asked, "on my way to this conference room, I noticed that we were passing by the planet, Neptune. Are we leaving our solar system?"

Understanding that this group just experienced a horrific trauma, Thia reassuringly smiled at Gunther, and replied, "yes we are. We are headed to the Sombrero Galaxy which is almost 30 million light years from our present location."

"That is 29.35 million light years; to be exact," said Doctor Beckman.

Thia nodded at Doctor Beckman, and said, "for those of you who don't know our chief scientist, let me introduce you to Doctor Beckman—or Beck—as we lovingly call him."

Beck blushed and pushed his thick, horn-rimmed glasses up the bridge of his nose.

"Beck, after this meeting is over and after Gunther gets settled in, I would like you to familiarize him with the ship."

Beck nodded.

Before Thia continued with the briefing, Gunther raised his hand again, and asked, "how long will it take us to get to the Sombrero Galaxy? Thirty million light years is an impossible distance for a lifetime."

"Two weeks," Beck said with a smirk.

Knowing that Gunther wasn't satisfied with that answer, Thia quickly said, "Gunther, I am so happy to have someone of your engineering abilities in our community. Beck will give you a detailed briefing of our ship's drive and propulsion systems which will answer your questions."

Understanding that Thia politely dismissed any further discussions about the workings of the ship, Gunther sat back in his chair with a frown.

"Now to continue," Thia said, "as your engineer, Gunther, astutely observed, we are leaving our solar system.

154

Soon we will be departing the *Local Galactic Cluster* which our galaxy, *The Milky Way*, resides. Once we leave the Milky Way Galaxy, we will travel to the *Virgo Galactic Cluster*. The *Sombrero Galaxy* resides in this cluster. In the Sombrero Galaxy there is the planet: Zenti. That will be your new home."

Thia paused, looked around the room as well as the view screen and seeing no questions, continued, "our South Dakota colony—which once consisted of approximately two-thousand individuals—grew in numbers during our initial journey. Before we departed the Milky Way Galaxy, we added about four hundred individuals from Apollo's planet: Delphi. Then about a year ago we found out that Earth was doomed. Because of the nuclear wars that ensued after my South Dakota colony departed; Earth was thrown out of its original orbit which caused the Moon to lose its orbital cohesion. Initially, Earth and its moon enjoyed a gravitational balance. However, the enormous pounding that Earth endured due to repeated, nuclear detonations created a gravitational imbalance between the two celestial bodies causing the Earth to exert a greater pull on the Moon. Upon finding this out, we built more ships and luckily rescued almost ten thousand souls from Earth before the Moon crashed into its surface making it uninhabitable."

Thia paused. Knowing that most of the Martian colonists knew nothing about both the nuclear explosions and the subsequent destruction of Earth—she expected to be bombarded with questions—but none came.

"So," she continued, "our Zentian community consists of mostly Earthlings—from all over the planet— some Dephians and one entity from a region of Space that we call: *The Black Expanse.*"

Thia paused again. Then not hearing any questions, she continued.

"Finally, when we were alerted to Mars' possible destruction and knew that Earthlings colonized the planet, we launched a rescue mission." Thia paused and waited for questions. Again, none were asked.

Hearing no concerns about her narrative, Thia continued, and said, "now, as I mentioned previously, your Martian colonists will be broken into smaller groups and given a ship's guide. The guide will assign you living quarters, give you a tour of the ship, and see to your overall wellbeing. And, more importantly, the guide can answer any further questions you might have."

Thia looked at everyone around the room then directly at the view screen, and said, "welcome to the Zentian community."

With those words, the meeting ended. As Thia stood, Fly approached her carrying Fritzie who sat on his lap during the briefing. He nodded at Fritzie while not taking his eyes off Thia, and said, "Miss Thia, you have a very special little man here."

Thia took Fritzie from Fly's arms and comfortably rested him on her hip. Even though she disliked the fuss Pythia made upon first meeting her, she liked the title of respect Fly used: *Miss*. During her last reincarnation as an African American woman on Earth, that title was always a term of endearment.

Then looking at Cheryl, who was at Fly's side, she said, "you are a very special young man, Fly. You are welcome to spend time with Fritzie if you like."

CHAPTER 2

After everyone was assigned rooms and roommates of their choosing, both Cheryl and Pythia found themselves sitting together in a luxurious living room sipping glasses of red wine.

"Can you believe how spacious these living quarters are?" Cheryl exclaimed while looking around at their chosen two-bedroom apartment.

Pythia sipped her wine, smiled, and said with a keen eye, "I would say that these apartments are definitely scaled up from ours in Bio-2."

Cheryl nodded in agreement.

"I am so happy to have *you* as a roommate," Pythia said. "Don't get me wrong—I enjoyed living with Alicia on Mars—however, living with an adult is refreshing."

Cheryl nodded, and said, "agreed. It seems like Fly, Otto and Gregory decided to room together for the next two weeks. And, from my simple understanding of this ship, their apartment resides in the other orb that has living quarters."

Pythia laughed, and said, "both Alicia and Heather are rooming together and living in that same orb."

"I guess—whether we like it or not—it's time our children flew the coop," Cheryl said somberly.

In silence, Cheryl noticed how her friend had changed. She could not quite put a finger on it. There was something different in Pythia's eyes perhaps? After a few moments of silence and a couple sips of wine, Cheryl asked, "so, this *Thia*? Why did you bow to her? And how is she Apollo's sister? They look nothing alike."

Pythia always felt comfortable in Cheryl's company; comfortable enough to tell her the whole truth. And now that they departed the solar system, she knew who *she* really was. Images of all her past lives flooded through her mind.

"Well," Pythia began, "we all heard of Apollo; he is the god of prophecy, light, music, and much more."

Remembering how unsettled she felt when standing next to Apollo, Cheryl simply nodded.

"Most of the Greek myths are true only they did not occur on Earth, but on a planet called Delphi. There are gods such as Zeus, Hera, Ares, Apollo, and many more. Just like there are gods on Delphi there are other beings called muses. Muses are beautiful beings. They have inspired art and beauty throughout the ages. These muses are visible on the moon, Cyn, that orbits a Gas Giant planet not far from the Delphian system of planets."

159

From the little Cheryl knew about Greek mythology, she knew that muses were the creators of great beauty.

"So," Pythia continued, "there is a Mount Olympus on Delphi which is inhabited by the Olympic gods. As a young girl, I studied under an oracle in the city of Helenes which is located only a few miles from Mount Olympus. I was about seventeen when I became a priestess to Apollo. At that time, Apollo was a young boy. Although young, Apollo was able to use me as an instrument for his prophecies."

Even though Cheryl thought that Pythia's story was strange, she silently listened.

"Both Apollo and his sister, Thia, were sired by Zeus. However, their mothers were not Olympians; they were muses from the moon, Cyn. Thia's and Apollo's mothers are Dionne and Leto, respectively. When I initially met Thia, she looked like Apollo—fair skin, blue eyes, and blond hair."

After a gulp of wine, Cheryl shook her head, and asked, "are you talking about reincarnation?"

Pythia nodded, and continued, "the story gets better from here. Zeus was married to his sister, Hera. Since Thia was conceived from one of Zeus' infidelities, Hera plotted to have her removed from Mount Olympus. Because Hera rained cruelties on the commoners, Thia started an uprising against the gods. When the uprising failed, under Olympian law, Thia had to be put to death. However, Zeus could not bring himself to kill his beloved daughter, so he banished her and ten-thousand others to be exiled to Earth. At that time, primitive Neanderthals roamed Earth. It was a hell of a planet."

160

Cheryl narrowed her eyes trying to put this whole story and its timeline into perspective, and said, "that had to be over twenty-thousand years ago—maybe longer. But you said that Apollo was a young boy on Delphi when his sister was exiled. Why does Apollo look like he is in his mid-thirties?"

"Time on Delphi passes differently than on Earth," Pythia replied. "Anyhow, I was also exiled along with Thia and the others. We interbred with the Neanderthal, grew civilizations, and thrived. However, through time and Earth's harsh environment, our bodies disintegrated; but our souls did not."

Cheryl stood, grabbed the opened bottle of red wine from the kitchenette, poured both a heaping glass full, and asked, "you are talking again about reincarnation?"

Pythia nodded, and replied, "yes. However, with each reincarnation, I forgot who I was. But what is curious, I still gravitated towards those tied to the natural world."

"You mean like being a veterinarian and having a history of your family associated with shamans?"

Pythia smiled.

"So," Cheryl continued, "even though the Thia that we see today is an African American woman in her mid-twenties, tens of thousands of Earth years ago she was a fair-skinned blond; just like in the Greek myths."

Pythia scanned the digital clock display that was part of the apartment's wall and announced, "that reminds me. We are expected at Thia's apartment tonight for a dinner party."

161

CHAPTER 3

"This is one hell of a spaceship you have here," Gunther said to Beck as they stood in the astrophysics laboratory.

"As I said before, I can't take all the credit for it," Beck insisted.

Gunther shook his head in disbelief, and said, "I know, I know, you said that your children built this marvel. I am having a hard time wrapping my head around that."

The two men stood over a lab table where the spaceship's holographic, three-dimensional blueprints were displayed. At a quick glance, Gunther noticed that the diagram consisted of seven large balls. Upon further inspection, he saw that these balls occupied different vertical levels. Three balls sat on the bottom level and were connected by long cylinders which essentially formed a triangle. This pattern was similar

162

for the second level. The third level was occupied by one ball which was floating in the center of the opposing triangles. Gunther also noticed that these seven balls were enclosed in a transparent bubble.

"First, I will briefly explain the layout of the ship," Beck began referring to the blueprints. "And, next we can go to the engine room and I will give you an overview of our propulsion and drive systems."

Eager to understand the intricacies of this astonishing ship, Gunther enthusiastically nodded.

Looking at the holographic blueprints, Beck began, "these balls, or as we call them: *orbs*, which occupy the bottom level, contain our engines, smaller shuttles, fighter ships, and scientific laboratories. The cylindrical connecting tubes, which we call: *Benta Tubes,* are just that; they provide a walkway to the individual orbs." Next, Beck pointed to the middle group of orbs. "Two of these are our habitat orbs. There are over two-thousand apartments located there. Besides apartments, these orbs contain a park with trees and streams that is located at the bottom. The third orb that makes up this mid-level triangle is a recreational orb. It contains lounges, cafeterias, recreational rooms, forests, rangelands, and so forth."

Although he was eager for the briefing to continue, Gunther asked, "rangelands?"

"Yes." Beck replied. "We had many animals to take along with us on the first ship we built; the one we used to escape from Earth. These rangelands came in handy when we

163

rescued other Earthlings who had livestock. Even with your Martian colony, we were able to bring all of your animals along."

Gunther was astounded by the careful planning that went into building this spaceship. He wanted to know more, he said, "please continue."

Beck now pointed to the last orb that sat above the bottom six, and said, "as you can guess by now, this orb is where our Bridge resides. Not only is the command center for the ship located on this orb, but there are also meeting places for large parties, the map room, various small parks, and a weapons' arsenal."

The two men remained silent while Gunther tried to absorb the spaceship's intricacies. He simply smiled to himself when he thought that the spaceship, which he flew to Mars, was a work of engineering genius. However, while viewing the intricacies of this spaceship, his Martian ship was akin to a horse and carriage. Never in his lifetime did he imagine traveling on such a magnificent vessel.

"So," Gunther finally said, "each of these orbs are one mile in diameter. And the configuration of all seven orbs consist of a five-mile diameter cluster."

Beck nodded.

"And your electromagnetic shield," Gunther said while referring the transparent bubble that encapsulated all seven orbs, "is approximately five miles in diameter."

Beck nodded.

"Magnificent!" Gunther complimented. "And you said that the ship is outfitted with teleportation closets?"

Beck smiled, and said, "that is correct. Throughout the ship there are teleportation hubs. These are like elevators only they will deconstruct your molecular makeup, transport you to your desired location, and reconstruct you before the door opens."

"If you have those devices, then why do you need *Benta Tubes*?

"Those tubes are not only walkways, but they also provide structural integrity to the ship," Beck explained.

Beck nodded towards the lab's exit, and said, "let us go to the engine room and I will explain our propulsion and drive systems."

With all this new engineering information swirling around his head, Gunther simply followed Beck's lead as they exited the laboratory.

CHAPTER 4

"I know that I am just a lowly engineer and not some exalted theoretical scientist, but I thought that the *Theory of Relativity* prohibits anyone from traveling faster than the speed of light," Gunther challenged.

Beck had been in this argument many times previous. However, as a professor, he enjoyed the teaching aspect of such debates; so, he said, "yes. You are correct. The *Theory of Relativity* states that faster-than-light travel is impossible because as an object approaches light-speed, its mass becomes infinitely heavy. Thus, taking an infinite amount of power to obtain that speed. An amount of power that we currently don't have access to."

"Very well then, Professor, how are we traveling at light-speed?" Gunther asked.

Readjusting his glasses—pushing them up the bridge of his nose—Beck replied, "we ignore *that* theory. That theory was derived on Earth. As you well know, Space has its own laws that are quite different from the laws that apply on Earth." Then using a tried-and-true teaching tool to back up his statements, Beck walked over to a plant that decorated an office in the engine room, ripped off a small leaf that was no bigger than the size of his palm, and held it up to his eye. "You see this leaf?" He asked.

Gunther nodded.

Beck walked back to Gunther's side and handed him the leaf. After the leaf was in Gunther's possession, he paced thirty feet from the engineer, and instructed, "now throw the leaf to me."

Gunther looked at the delicate vegetation, frowned, and asked, "what does a leaf have to do with the speed of light?"

"Throw it," Beck commanded.

Gunther huffed and threw the leaf with all his strength. He shook his head in disgust as he watched the delicate vegetation move upward and forward and land only two feet from him.

Beck smirked, and said, "bring the leaf here."

Gunther retrieved the leaf then handed it to Beck. Beck took the leaf from Gunther, secured it inside a small glass bottle, and handed Gunther the bottle.

"Now," said Beck, "go back to where you were standing before and throw the leaf which is now encased in that bottle."

167

Gunther did as Beck instructed and this time the bottle reached Beck.

Humbly, Gunther nodded at Beck, and said, "the spaceship's electromagnetic shield is the bottle. Isn't it?"

"Yes, our ship is encased in an electromagnetic shield made of *photons* that both allows us to surf the atmosphere of Space at light speeds and protects us from time dilation effects. Like the leaf, without the shield, we cannot go faster than the speed of light no matter how much energy we use to accelerate. However, since the shield is made of the same environment as Space, we are simply surfing at speeds that are normal to its environment."

Gunther scratched his head, and asked, "are you talking about laws in *Quantum Physics*?"

Beck nodded, and replied, "I guess you want to know about our energy source next?"

Although Gunther was a tried-and-true engineer, he loved all science and welcomed the chance to learn more.

"That's why I am here," Gunther said with a smirk.

"Our propulsion system is based on *negative matter*," Beck said.

After hearing this, Gunther remained silent. He heard the debates about types of matter. Scientists debated that future propulsion systems could use *anti-matter* to propel ships through Space. However, with present technology, there simply was not a method to contain it. Very few scientists spoke of *negative matter*. He knew, in Newtonian Physics, that a force is equal to a mass multiplied by its acceleration. He knew that if one forcefully threw a ball towards the floor that it would react by bouncing in the opposite direction. It would bounce back into the hands of the thrower. He also knew that the ball and the floor were made of *positive matter*. However, with *negative matter*, when the ball strikes the floor, it does not bounce back but picks up more energy and continues. It burrows through the floor.

"I have heard debates about this type of matter," Gunther said. "If we were somewhere on the North American continent and I bounced a ball that consisted of *negative matter*—it would bore its way through the floor and all the way to China then into Space while all the time picking up speed with each surface of resistance."

Beck remained silent.

"So," said Gunther, "this spaceship doesn't need fuel. If we want to accelerate, we find some resistance that will increase our speed through Space. And, once an object in Space is accelerated to a given speed, it can glide forever at that speed with its trajectory affected only by the force of gravity emanating from planets and such."

Beck smiled and nodded.

"Now I see the genius in this spaceship's design," Gunther said. "At first, when you showed me the spaceship's three-dimensional, holographic schematics, I thought the design quite bulky with these large orbs which are each one-mile in diameter. That is not very aerodynamic. Now, I understand that since we need resistance for propulsion and that a ball-shaped object hits more resistance than a needle-shaped object, this design is perfect for a *negative matter propulsion system.* The more resistance, the farther we propel forward."

"Excellent!" Beck praised. "You, my dear engineer, will make a fine addition to our Zentian scientific community."

CHAPTER 5

The *Red Lounge*, located in the recreational orb, was full of patrons. It was decorated with a bar that lined one wall and over thirty tables littered throughout. Even though the lighting was soothing, the walls were completely transparent allowing its patrons a view of the cosmos. Littered with far-off, seemingly stationary stars and massive, distant, gas clouds; the cosmos' near-window view blurred with streaks of nearby stars as the spaceship zoomed by.

Heather, Otto, and Gregory were seated around a table next to the transparent wall while Fly and Alicia were at the bar getting drinks for the table.

While standing at the bar, Alicia saw that the two bartenders were no older than their group of friends. The first one to catch her eye looked native to the American continent just like her.

As he handed her a tray filled with beers, Alicia asked, "I hope not to offend you, but are you Native American?"

The slender bartender with his shoulder-length hair pulled back in a ponytail, winked at Alicia, and replied, "my family is from the Black Hills of South Dakota. I am a Sioux Indian."

Alicia nodded, and said, "my family is from El Salvador. I am from a long-line of Mayans."

"I am aware of your Native American heritage. We know who we are," the young man said. "My name is Zeke Hawkfeather."

"I am Alicia," she introduced.

Taking in this information, Fly asked the other bartender, who now handed him a tray of snacks, "are you from South Dakota also?"

The young, dark-brown-skinned teen shyly smiled, and replied, "not at all. I am from the planet, Delphi. And Apollo is my patron god."

"That is awesome," Fly said. "My name is Fly. And I am from Earth—a place called the United States."

"I am Pulo," the bartender responded.

After Fly and Alicia returned to their table, they placed the two trays at its center.

"Hey, those two bartenders," Fly said to the group as he nodded his head towards the bar, "they want to hang with us sometime later."

"They are certainly people we should get to know," Alicia said. After a sip of her beer, she first looked at the

172

panoramic view of Space provided by the lounge's transparent walls then looked at the faces of her friends, and exclaimed, "can you guys believe this incredible spaceship?"

Remembering the windowless, cramped conditions on the spaceship that took him from Earth to Mars, Gregory said, "initially, I thought that our scientists and engineers designed a modern marvel. Now, being on this magnificent ship…". Gregory paused while trying to explain his amazement. "I have no words to describe it," he concluded spouting a large grin.

Almost everyone at the table was silent as they drank their beers while transfixing their gaze on the amazing views of Space. Heather, however, solemnly stared at her beer. Aware of Heather's sadness, Alicia said, "I know we've danced around the subject since we watched the catastrophe unfold on Mars, but I do recognize that you two lost family members during that horrid event."

Heather looked up from her beer, gazed into Alicia's comforting eyes, and remained silent.

"Thank you for those kind words," Gregory said. "I tried my best to get them to come along, but they were arrogant and stubborn."

Heather, now staring out the window, remained silent.

Gregory looked at each of his friends, and said, "they were on borrowed time anyway. They got what they deserved."

Even though Heather knew that the aristocrats were harvesting organs from the Bio-2 teens, she still missed her family and began to cry. She stood up in one swift move and with a trembling voice she said to Gregory, "I still miss them."

When Heather began to walk away from them, Alicia stood and started to go after her. However, Gregory gently pulled Alicia back into her seat.

Gregory took another deep breath, and said to his friends, "you may think that I am cruel. However, I must tell you why I said that both of our families got what they deserved. Heather and I found out that our parents were killing teens from Bio-2 and harvesting their organs."

Shocked by this news, no one spoke.

"If you remember the rules of the talent contest," Gregory continued. "They stated that whoever won the contest was offered an apartment in Bio-1 or a trip back to Earth. And, when I found my dead brother's diary which chronicled the destruction of Earth, I became suspicious. Another thing, during our investigation we could not find a trace of the previous winners. And, since they did not go to Earth, we knew that something terrible happened to them. Finally, it was Heather who put the pieces together about organ harvesting. Several of our relatives, who were previously sick, were recipients of those organs."

Otto became angered by this news.

"Fly and I could have been the next donors," Otto raged. "Were you going to tell us about your findings?"

Gregory nodded, and replied, "of course I was. But the volcanic event happened so fast that I didn't have a chance."

Otto, who was seated across from Gregory, leaned across the table, grabbed Gregory by the collar, and said, "no. You were not going to tell us about these criminal acts. You were going to let us die."

Seeing Otto's balled fist about to smash Gregory in the face, Fly immediately stood, got between the two strapping teens, and pried Otto's other fist from Gregory's collar. After Gregory's collar was released, his body's counterforce thrust him back into his chair.

Next, Fly forced Otto back into his chair, sat next to him, and said, "he is telling us about this now. Gregory didn't have to tell us anything since we are all safe in this ship."

Otto just sat in his chair and brooded.

"Fly is right," Alicia said. "Gregory told me about the organ-harvesting scheme the other night. And, he would have told you two if the disaster didn't strike."

Red-faced, Otto growled, stood up then left the table.

Fly also stood, and said, "I going to talk some sense into my friend."

Alone with Gregory, Alicia said, "come on, let's go stand near the window and enjoy this incredible space-scape!"

Gregory reluctantly nodded.

CHAPTER 6

That evening, everyone on the ship was informed that they were close to the Milky Way Galaxy's center. Dr. Beckman briefed the entire ship's complement regarding the massive, black hole which occupied the galaxy's center. After Beck gave a highly scientific explanation to the Martian colonists, Thia's face appeared on every view screen.

"As Beck informed everyone, we are now approaching the Milky Way's black hole. And there is nothing to be alarmed about. Our spaceship has shields that will allow us to not only get close to the black hole's Event Horizon—its outer boundary—but will also ensure safe passage through the phenomenon. We managed this maneuver twice in the past with no harmful incidences. Since this may be a once-in-a-lifetime event for most of you, I suggest that wherever you are on the ship that you go to one of the windows. It is a view of a lifetime!"

After listening to Thia's voice while enjoying a glass of wine at the Red Lounge, Cheryl finished the wine, stood up, and walked to its wrap-around window. Looking through the transparent hull, she saw a massive oval of darkness ahead.

"Would you like a drink?" Apollo asked as he appeared at her side with an offering of red wine.

Startled, Cheryl looked up into the smooth-skinned face of this curly-haired *Adonis* who stood next to her. Not only did his sudden appearance disturb her, but she *felt* him. She felt some invisible force that extended from his physical body. A powerful force that pulled on everything inside of her. Her heart raced, her brain scattered, and her skin tingled all over.

"I have seen this event twice in the past. It is truly remarkable!" Apollo said with a smile as he handed her a glass of wine.

Cheryl showed courage all her life when faced with imminent danger. This was no different. So, taking a deep breath to steady her racing heart, she took the drink from his hand, nodded graciously, and turned towards the view ahead.

Apollo sipped wine from his glass as he stood next to Cheryl. Never in his long life had he been so enchanted. There was something mysterious about this earth-woman. Was it her aura? Was it her scientific, logical mind? Was it that she looked like his sister incarnate? Or was it her shyness? He could not quite understand the enchantment. However, he wanted to get to know her.

177

"Do you see that aura surrounding the black hole?" Apollo asked hoping to draw out Cheryl's interest.

Cheryl looked at the black hole that lay in their path. From a distance, she saw what looked like a sunflower. Like a sunflower, she saw a massive black ball, or seed, surrounded by yellow leaves. However, unlike a sunflower, not only was there a cone of light that shot from the center of the seed, but also there was a thin, transparent shield—like an atmosphere—encasing the seed. Cheryl knew *why* the seed was black. She knew that because of the black hole's massive gravity, that anything near it, even light, was devoured. But that was all she knew about black holes.

Avoiding looking directly at Apollo, Cheryl focused her gaze at the phenomenon, and asked, "you mean that thin, atmospheric-like layer?"

"Yes," Apollo nodded. "Well, that is the black hole's Event Horizon. It prevents things from escaping."

"Dr. Beckman said that the Event Horizon will help us go faster? I just don't understand that."

"Yes, it will propel us," Apollo answered again. "The genius in this spaceship's design is that after it hits resistance, it accelerates. Then, upon broaching the Event Horizon, we will have so much resistance that the ship will be propelled to a speed of millions-of-light-years per day."

Cheryl remained silent as she digested this information. Then after a few seconds, she asked, "I thought that nothing could escape a black hole—not even light—that's why it is black."

"You are correct again," Apollo said. "However, light travels at a specific speed. We will be traveling much, much faster than light after we hit that barrier. Think of the black-hole's gravity as a human being and our ship as a freight train. The human being tries to stop the freight train when it passes by, but no matter how much that person holds on to the train's back railing and digs his heels into the ground after he grabs the train, he cannot stop it. Thus, upon encountering that barrier, the black-hole's gravitational forces cannot keep us within it. And the spaceship's sophisticated, electromagnetic shield will protect us."

Again, Cheryl remained silent while she absorbed the information. Then, feeling more relaxed for the first time since Apollo stood next to her, she looked at him with an engaging smile.

"So, you're not just a good-looking god; you are also a scientist as well," she teased.

Cheryl's comment rocked Apollo. Inwardly, he became wobbly; a little less self-assured. This time he forced himself to peel his eyes away from Cheryl and stare out the window.

"I dabble," he responded.

Now feeling almost comfortable, Cheryl smiled, and said, "so, tell me more about the black hole. What is that yellow halo surrounding it? What is that stream of light shooting from its middle?"

"The yellow halo surrounding it is called an Accretion Disc. This disc is composed of super-heated gas and dust that whirl around the black hole at immense speeds producing

179

electromagnetic radiation such as X-rays and infrared rays. And the stream of light that is shooting from its middle is called a Relativistic Jet."

"Relativistic Jet," Cheryl repeated.

"Yes. A black hole feeds on stars, gasses, and dust. While digesting this meal, bursts of particles and radiation jet out. Some of these jets stretch light years."

"Like a massive burp!" Cheryl chuckled.

Apollo nodded and laughed.

While watching the speedway of the Accretion Disc and the dancing particle stream of the Relativistic Jet, Cheryl did not notice that the entire lounge became bathe in the glow of X-rays that streamed from the jets.

Then it happened. In the moments that passed between the time the spaceship contacted the Event Horizon and its blinding acceleration to incredible, light speeds, Cheryl turned to face Apollo. She was shocked by what she saw. The bathing radiation set his body aglow. His skin was fiery and shiny; almost luminous. He now sported a glow that encapsulated his entire body. His previous blue eyes now became a radiant yellow and his blond hair floated around his head. Apollo resembled no creature Cheryl had seen before.

Similarly, Apollo saw Cheryl clearly for the first time. She too had changed while bathe in the radiative glow. Her previously warm, brown eyes became jet black like the universe. And, like the universe, these jet-black pools were speckled with white-hot stars! Her previously dark-brown skin

180

darkened even more to the color of indigo. And her entire body was surrounded by a sparkling mesh.

On his previous trips to the center of the Milky Way Galaxy, he had never seen anyone transform like that. And even though he could not understand what he saw, he had to touch her. So, with a steady hand, he reached out and touched the sparkling mesh that surrounded Cheryl. When he made contact, a surge of energy burst through the two of them.

Feeling this energy surge, Cheryl was not afraid. She closed her eyes and took slow, deep breaths. Apollo, on the other hand, was a bit frightened. This was something new for him. This was a feeling that no Olympian god could describe.

CHAPTER 7

The following morning, the teenagers voraciously ate breakfast at the Blue Lounge. Not only was the food tastier than their food on Mars, but it was also plentiful.

After taking a sip of coffee, Heather said, "this spaceship is *spooky*."

Before anyone asked Heather to explain her statement, an eighteen-year-old waitress appeared at their table. This exotic beauty's facial features were a cultural mixture of ancestries from Asia and Europe.

Promptly attending to her duties, the waitress asked, "may I refill your coffees?"

Fly took in the presence of this beauty, and answered for everyone, "yes, please."

While the waitress filled the coffee cups, Fly said, "since none of the Martian colonists are working aboard this ship, I assume that you are either from Earth's South Dakota colony or from the planet, Delphi."

The waitress smiled as she continued to fill the coffee cups.

When no answer came, Fly eyed her from head to toe and continued, "my bet is that you are from the South Dakota colony."

After topping off the last coffee cup, the waitress stood up straight and looked Fly square in the eyes. With a dazzling smile, she said, "that was my home before we escaped Earth."

Momentarily stunned silent by the waitress' charm, Fly collected himself, and said, "then, you must know Zeke Hawkfeather."

The waitress nodded, and said, "yes, he is my best friend."

"We met both Zeke and Pulo last night," Alicia chimed in. "They offered to show us around the ship. By the way, my name is Alicia."

"Stephanie," the waitress nodded her head. "My name is Stephanie."

"Would you accompany all of us on the tour?" Fly asked.

"It just depends on my work schedule," Stephanie replied. "In the meantime, I suggest that you guys wander around and have a look for yourselves. That way when we all get together, you can ask more specific questions."

With those words, Stephanie certainly got the teenagers attention. Everyone at the table had questions. Questions

183

about the ship, about the South Dakota colony, and, more importantly, about their new home-world: Zenti. However, before they had a chance to ask any questions a person from a nearby table got her attention by pointing at his empty, coffee cup.

"Got to go," Stephanie said with a wink.

After Stephanie walked away, Heather continued the initial conversation which everyone else forgot about. "This ship is *spooky*. Spooky like that Stephanie."

Otto shook his head while he swallowed down a heaping spoonful of scrambled eggs. After the eggs were safely down his throat, he asked, "what are you talking about?"

Heather leveled Otto a serious look, and replied, "I said that this ship is spooky. The ship is spooky like that Stephanie girl. She just appeared at our table."

"Duh! That is what servers do," Otto insisted.

Heather shook her head, and said, "of course, that is what servers do. But one minute she wasn't here and the next she was."

Alicia was concerned about the wellbeing of her roommate. Just within the last week, Heather lost her entire family. Alicia remembered how hard she fell when her father died in the tragic accident that also took the lives of Otto's mother, Fly's father, and Gregory's brother. She knew that such a loss could devastate one's mental wellbeing. Alicia remembered that it helped that she had her mother to mourn with. Heather has no one.

184

"You know, Heather," Alicia began, "while we were all eating our breakfast, I think we were so absorbed in this wonderful feast that perhaps we weren't aware *when* Stephanie came to the table," she reasoned.

"Okay," Heather conceited, "maybe so. But, what about that Apollo guy?"

"He is certainly different," Fly answered. "They explained to us about Delphi; that's where he is from."

"And" Alicia added, "Fly and I met a Delphian last night at the bar. He seems normal."

Heather's face reddened. She could not understand why her friends accepted this new reality. "Apollo is a myth! Why is a *myth* walking around this ship? And, what about that scary baby?"

"Fritzie?" Fly asked.

Heather nodded.

Fly liked the toddler. "He's just a child."

With those words, everyone became silent. Both Gregory and Alicia remembered the prophetically soothing dreams they had of the toddler. They both knew that the calming image of the toddler eased them through the horrific past few days.

Alicia brooded. "Yeah, he is a child; and a creepy one at that."

Everyone remained silent.

"What about the fact that people are either changing or missing?"

185

Gregory blinked a few times while trying to understand not only Heather's words but also her train of thought.

"Heather, what do you mean by changing or missing?" Gregory asked.

"Well after we passed by the center of our galaxy and the ship was flooded with some x-ray type light, several of my friends—some from yoga class—went missing and a few of the other ones had weird looks on their faces."

"You mean when we went pass galaxy's black hole?" Otto asked.

Heather nodded.

"Wasn't that exciting," Otto continued while completely ignoring Heather's concern. Then looking directly at his buddy, Fly, he added, "my father explained this to me. He said that Doctor Beckman told him that for the ship to travel at a speed of millions-of-lightyears per day that we had to fly through the Event Horizon of the Milky Way's black hole. This massive impact would activate the *negative matter* propulsion system to accelerate us to that speed."

Fly politely smiled. He did not understand what Otto was saying just like he did not understand Doctor Beckman's explanation during the event.

"Guys," Alicia said softly, "let us get back to Heather's point."

Alicia understood that her mother had changed since they were on the ship. Whenever she saw her mother, she noticed that her mother's eyes had a trans-like, far-off look. Just like the look in Fly's eyes.

186

"What? Why are you staring at me?" Fly asked Alicia.

Alicia shook off the musing. She realized that she was staring solely at Fly, and replied, "nothing. I was just thinking."

"I think," Heather began, "that this is a *Ghost Ship*. I think that we all died on Mars and now are on the ship of the dead."

Although Gregory felt that Heather's thinking was completely irrational, he empathized with her. He knew that everything which kept her stable: her family, her social status, and her dignity was ripped from her like a bandage from an unhealed wound. He needed to help her. He needed to divert her attention from the past few days as well as help her heal.

"I say we take Stephanie's advice," Gregory said as he looked at each person around their breakfast table. "After we are done eating, let us take a tour of the ship."

Everyone agreed—even Heather.

187

CHAPTER 8

When Cheryl and Pythia arrived at Thia's apartment, they found that Gunther, Doctor Beckman, and Apollo were already there.

The two women were not only greeted by the hostess, but also a very inviting aroma.

"Yummy," said Cheryl as she stood in the doorway, "whatever you are cooking smells delicious."

Clothed in a floor-length casual dress with her hair piled upon the top of her head, Thia greeted both women with a welcoming smile, and said, "please come in and make yourself at home. The meal that my brother and I prepared is steeped in traditions from African American, Lakota Sioux, and Delphian Greek."

After Cheryl and Pythia found seats on the sofa, Apollo walked from the bedroom brandishing a smile, and announced,

"Fritzie is officially asleep! Now, I can take over my bartending duties." Looking over the guests he noticed the two new arrivals, and asked, "what can I get for you lovely ladies?"

With drinks in hand, Thia motioned that everyone should sit at the table. The middle of the table was lined with dish after inviting dish.

Cheryl gladly went to the table and began serving herself.

After everyone was again seated with a plate of food and their drink of choice, Thia raised her glass, and said, "I would like to propose a toast to new friends and family."

Gunther, who sat next to Thia, drank from his beer mug then requested, "Apollo, tell me about your people. I particularly want to know how you managed to contact our Martian colony from across the universe without any devices other than dreams?"

After a long sip of wine, Apollo said, "well, on my father's side, my sister and I come from a long line of nine-dimensional beings."

Gunther shook his head and blinked his eyes while trying to understand what he was hearing.

Seeing that their dinner guests, except for Beck, were totally confused, Apollo continued by asking "how do you think of time?"

Gunther thought that a stupid question. But, for the sake of conversation, he answered, "we all know that time is composed of seconds, minutes, hours, days, and so forth."

"So, for you," Apollo reasoned, "you are born, you live, and you die?"

Gunther nodded in agreement, and asked, "doesn't everyone?"

"Not necessarily," Apollo answered. "Your concept of time is quite linear. Is it not?"

"Of course," Gunther replied.

"So," Apollo continued, "as dimensional beings, you Earthlings live in four dimensions: length, width, height, and time. And you move through time on a linear scale?"

Gunther swallowed more beer and replied, "yes. Certainly!"

Seeing that he had everyone at the table engaged in the conversation, Apollo beamed, and continued, "to Olympians, time isn't linear. Time has three dimensions—the past, the present, and the future. Our three-dimensional bodies can instantaneously exist in all three dimensions of time."

After swallowing a spoon of wild rice infused with pine nuts and cranberries, Pythia eyes widened, and she asked, "is that how you are able to tell the future?"

Apollo sweetly smiled at his priestess and nodded his head.

"Of course, it takes practice and discipline to move through time dimensions," Thia chimed in. "And, although every Olympian has the ability to experience all three dimensions of time at once, my brother is one of the few who perfected this practice."

190

While slowly getting a grasp of Apollo's explanation, Gunther's heart raced as his face flushed. Gunther found this information too incredible. He looked around the table at everyone's faces. Seeing that they did not dispute Apollo's claim, he trained his stare solely on the non-Martian scientist at the table, Dr. Beckman, and asked, "do you believe this supernatural gibberish?"

Beck nodded, and replied, "It's true; all of it."

Gunther narrowed his eyes, stared at Apollo, and asked, "Okay, let us say that you Olympians are nine-dimensional beings; this only explains that you knew what the future would hold. However, it doesn't explain how you were able to contact us from halfway across the universe."

After cutting a piece of juicy chicken and chewing it into savory bits that slid down his throat, Apollo continued, "as I stated previously, both my sister and I are nine-dimensional beings on our father's side. However, both our mothers are muses. They are abstract beings. When Thia's mother, Dione, felt the universe slipping into *Chaos* which was extinguishing the light of *Clarity,* she devised a plan where we helped *Clarity* gain a firmer foothold in our known universe."

Seeing the confusion and disbelief on their guests' faces, Beck said, "I know as scientist, this is beyond our realm of thinking. However, living is much more than seeing and touching; it is also being."

Pythia nodded. "There is more to living. As scientists we deal with data more than feelings—and I think that we just don't have all the data *on* our feelings."

"After *Clarity* gained a foothold," Apollo continued, "most of the beings living in the universe evolved."

"Evolved?" Cheryl asked with a look of incomprehension. "Why, you are nine-dimensional beings. How can you evolve even further?"

"We evolved to a state of thought," Thia replied. "Not only could we move through the three-dimensional space and time, but we became more like the muses who live in the abstract."

"But" said Cheryl shakily, "you don't look abstract."

"In an instant we can be solid, corporeal beings; and in another instant we can be simple energy, or pure thought," Thia replied.

"That's how you were able to communicate with us halfway across the universe?" Pythia asked.

"So, with this new ability to become *pure thought*, we also became beings living in ten-dimensions. We evolved into ten-dimensional beings," Thia concluded.

Everyone at the table was silent. They ate their food and drank their drinks without a word.

Finally, Cheryl asked, "what about us? If what you said is true and your mother brought *Clarity* to the universe, why haven't we evolved? Gunther, Pythia, and I are still four-dimensional beings."

Seeing that everyone was finished eating, Thia stood up, and said, "let us get comfortable in the living room. I am afraid these dinner table chairs lose their comfort after a while."

192

After everyone was seated comfortably, Beck said, "to answer your question, Cheryl, we found that there are still pockets of *Chaos* in the universe. The people who designed and built your Martian colony had greed and self-preservation in mind. *Clarity* can only enter when vessels are receptive."

"You are right," Pythia said. "I feel a change coming over me. I felt reborn since I've been on this spaceship." Then thinking about her daughter, Alicia, she asked, "can others be enlightened?"

"Absolutely," Thia chimed in. "As I mentioned before, we rescued almost ten-thousand people from Earth just before the Moon crashed into it. And, as of now, almost seven thousand of them have been enlightened."

"As I live and breathe," said Gunther slowly. "I am sitting in the presence of ten-dimensional beings. But what if I do not want to be enlightened? What if I like my life as it is?"

"That's the beauty of our Zentian community," Beck said. "Thia said that seven thousand are enlightened, and we have over twelve thousand in our community. So, about five-thousand individuals are living as they wish, some in cities and some in rural areas. And everyone is in respectful harmony."

CHAPTER 9

The next morning, Otto, Fly, and Gregory met at Alicia-and Heather's apartment for a light breakfast. After eating their morning meal, the teens began their unstructured, spaceship's tour. They debated whether to travel to various parts of the ship by teleport chamber or Benta Tubes. Unable to obtain a solid majority, they decided to travel by both means.

From the time they became passengers on the ship, they were mostly limited to the residential orbs. Since they explored the residential orbs on their own, they decided to see the remainder of the ship. The two orbs that were of immediate interest to the teens were the recreational and the Bridge orbs. Since the recreational orb contained lounges, cafeterias, recreation rooms, forests, rangelands, and so forth; they decided to take a Benta Tube to that orb and then from there to travel by means of a teleport hub to the spaceship's Bridge.

Standing in front of a circular opening to the Benta Tube, Fly waved his hand over a sensor. After the circular door slid open and disappeared into the spaceship's hull, the teens were shocked and awed by what they saw. Before them, lay the vastness of space. In the vista closest to the ship, they saw stars zooming by at lightening speeds. In the far vista they saw large, orange, yellow, and blue clouds of stellar nurseries.

Panicked by what she saw ahead of her, Heather shook her head in disbelief, and said, "I am not going in there. Where is the floor? Does it have oxygen?"

Otto nodded, and replied, "it is perfectly safe. It is just a walkway with transparent walls."

"That is the coolest thing I have ever seen!" Gregory said.

Heather began walking backwards while shaking her head. "No, I won't. I won't go to my death willingly on this *Ghost Ship.*"

Seeing that Heather was also physically scared by her trembling arms and legs, Fly put a comforting arm around her waist, and said to the others, "Heather and I will take the teleport and meet you guys on the recreational orb near the Red Lounge."

"Suit yourselves," Otto said as he gingerly stepped into the Benta Tube. After Alicia watched both Heather and Fly depart down the hall to the teleport hub, she followed Gregory as he stepped into the blackness of space. Upon entering the

195

tube and after the door to the residential orb closed, Alicia found herself disoriented. Except for the spaceship to her right, above, below and to her left was the view of the unknown. Even though she knew that her feet were positioned on a solid surface, she could not help but feel that at any moment she would be floating in the coldness of Space without breathable oxygen.

Suddenly, she felt warmth. Gregory stood at her side, grabbed her hand, and interlocked fingers. "Come with me sweetheart," he said tenderly.

Then, looking into Gregory's compassionate eyes while simultaneously feeling his warm hand interlaced with hers, she took a deep breath, smiled, and walked through the star-filled wonderland.

When the three teens emerged from the tube, they were exhilarated! With no words to describe their experience, they simply smiled in silence and headed towards the teleport device near the Red Lounge. After the five friends were together again, they toured the recreational orb. Since they had already seen the lounges, they walked by them and headed straight toward the recreation rooms. These rooms were typical of most gyms. They housed the usual treadmills, weight sets, and rowing machines in rooms lined with floor-to-ceiling mirrors. In other rooms they found spas complete with saunas and whirlpools.

"And look at this," said Alicia while staring, mouth agape, at an Olympic-sized, swimming pool.

Otto's eyes bulged in wonderment at this extravagant place, and he said, "never in my wildest dreams would I have imagined such a marvelous ship."

"Look Heather," Fly said as he watched people swimming, "see, there are people here."

After carefully looking at the sparse group of people recreating, Heather concluded, "these are people that I had seen, one time or another, at our Martian colony. Where are the Zentians?"

Alicia nodded in agreement, and said, "that is a good point. This place should be teeming with people that we *don't* know."

Aware that Alicia was echoing Heather's concerns about being on a *Ghost Ship*, Gregory—still holding Alicia's hand—said, "let's teleport to the Bridge. I am sure it is bustling with Zentians. And, if they allow us to enter the Bridge, we can ask for a tour."

Both Otto and Fly perked up. Always interested in how machines worked, the two young men nodded in agreement.

However, to his disappointment, Gregory's hopes were dashed after they stepped onto the Bridge. Even though he marveled at setup—the spaciousness, the large view screen that showed the space-scape ahead, the three command chairs that faced the screen, and the many computer stations complete with consoles and chairs that lined the walls; the Bridge was empty. Not a soul was there.

197

At this point, Heather began to sweat. Her hands and knees shook. "I told you!" She screamed. "This is a *Ghost Ship!*"

Otto looked around the empty Bridge. He knew that for such a large, complicated, galaxy-class spaceship there should be an equally large crew complement. "Where is the crew?" He calmly asked.

Seeing Heather's fear now reflecting in his friends' eyes, Fly smiled, and said, "hey guys, you need to calm down. For all we know, this ship is on autopilot."

Even though his words eased some of their fears, tension returned to the teens when Heather let out a cry, and said, "that creepy baby is here!"

Looking in the direction of Heather's stare, Fly saw Fritzie running up to him. Not knowing where Fritzie came from but looking down at the toddler standing next to him with open arms; Fly picked him up and rested him in his arms. "Hey little man," Fly said gently.

All eyes were trained on Fly and Fritzie as they watched the two smiling at each other. They were so taken with the sight that they did not notice when Stephanie, Thia, Zeke, and Pulo entered the Bridge.

Heather jumped with a startling cry when Thia spoke drawing their attention to the newcomers.

"I see you found the Bridge," Thia said.

Still shocked by the sudden appearance of the Zentians, Gregory shakily said, "yes. This is a marvelous ship you have here."

Thia nodded to Zeke and Stephanie, and said, "Zeke and Stephanie designed and built this ship."

Alicia's eyes widened while she said, "I thought you were a bartender and a waitress."

Zeke chuckled, and said, "we multitask."

"Would you guys like to see the transport and fighter vehicles?" Pulo asked.

"You too," said Heather shakily. "You're not just a bartender?"

"I am one of the pilots," Pulo answered proudly.

Seeing how overwhelmed Heather had become. And, knowing that this leap into the future was not for everyone, Thia walked to Heather's side, took her hand, and said, "come with us sweetie, we will help you adjust."

Frightened, Heather searchingly looked at her friends for help. When no one objected to Thia's suggestion, Heather then pleading scanned Thia's soft, inviting face, and asked, "us? Who is us?"

While still holding Heather's hand, Thia retrieved Fritzie from Fly with the other hand and rested him on her hip. "Why, Fritzie and I," she said while lovingly nodding to the toddler.

Although Heather was frightened by this new development, she saw only calm in her friends' faces. So, taking a deep breath, she allowed Thia to lead her into some sort of oblivion.

CHAPTER 10

After Thia and Heather exited the Bridge, Zeke took the group to the hangar area where a multitude of fighter vehicles and shuttle spacecrafts rested. Following the group's initial exploration of the vehicles, they headed to the Blue Lounge located on the recreational orb.

At the Blue Lounge, Gregory, Fly, Otto, Alicia, Pulo, and Zeke sat around the table as Stephanie approached them with a tray filled with beers. Even in the late afternoon, this lounge was bustling with patrons. Outside the windows, the same stars zoomed by on the blacken sky and the same, massive, gas clouds splashed across galaxies; inside was bright, cheery, and alive with excited voices.

Stephanie placed the heavy tray in the middle of the table, took the empty chair next to Zeke, and announced, "help yourselves."

Otto was the first to grab a beer. He was also the first to down a gulp. After the liquid slid down his throat and eased some tension, he asked, "how?" While looking around the lounge then looking at Zeke, he continued, "our best engineers built marvelous spaceships that carried us to Mars. And compared to this ship, our marvelous spaceships are merely skateboards. How could people like you build such a wonder?"

Zeke sat back in his chair trying to think of an explanation that would make sense to the group. However, before he explained, Stephanie said, "it took a village. Both Zeke and I, along with others, created the design. And, with the help of Doctor Beckman, our invention became reality. Furthermore, since the Black Hills had all the natural resources we needed to build this ship, the rest of the community helped in the manufacturing."

"Okay," said Otto after he downed another gulp of his drink, "that answers the nuts-and-bolts question of how the ship was built, but no engineer on Earth would even think of such a design. The ships' drive and propulsion systems along are mind blowing. Where did this inspiration come from?"

Gregory pensively scratched his head, and said, "I might have an inkling of where the inspiration came from," he said to Otto. "My brother's diary tells of rumors about an advanced group of people living in South Dakota. Moreover, his diary detailed that the United States government considered them anarchists. Furthermore, he alluded that through a miraculous event, this colony escaped the government's persecution and became space-bound." Gregory turned from

Otto and looked directly at Zeke, and asked, "and, back to Otto's point, how did you become so advanced that you could build such an amazing ship?"

"You all heard Apollo's story about how Thia and other Delphians—some Olympians and some commoners—were exiled to Earth during the Neanderthal time?" Zeke asked.

Otto, Alicia, Gregory, and Fly nodded simultaneously.

"Well, when they were exiled, Thia's mother, Dione, sent several of her family members to Earth to watch over them."

"Dione is a muse," Pulo stated.

"Aren't muses abstractions?" Alicia asked.

Pulo nodded, and replied, "although they live in pure energy form, they have the ability to interact with solid beings like us."

Initially, these muses watched over Thia's group while inspiring them in science, music, and art. That exiled group thrived," Stephanie said. "Although this group reincarnated through thousands of years, they always somehow found each other. And, more importantly, they all maintained their core intelligence. You may have heard of people from *Atlantis*."

Alicia eyes widened as she acknowledged the mythical civilization.

"Yes," Gregory said eagerly, "they were an advanced civilization that were leaps and bounds above our present civilization in science, math, music, and art."

Otto shook his head, "The operative word is *mythical*."

202

A grin spread across Fly's face, and he said, "from everything I've read, these Atlantians were not myths; they did exist."

"So," Zeke continued getting back to the explanation, "for thousands of years these muses watched over Thia's group through all of their reincarnations. However, over time, the muses lost their purpose and became corrupt."

Stephanie nodded, and added, "they changed from gentle watchers to power-hungry deities who demanded praise."

"Just like the Olympians on Delphi," Pulo added.

"Alerted to this change in the muses, Dione called them back one-by-one. However, not wanting to leave her beloved daughter unprotected, Dione not only left the youngest muse behind, but she also gave her enlightenment." Zeke said as he looked at each one around the table. "My people, the Sioux Indians of South Dakota, know her as the great spirit, *Wankatanka.*"

"Our inspiration came from her," Stephanie said. "And, *SHE* not only inspired us, but *SHE* also made sure that the everyone with the combination of Olympian and Muse bloodlines retained their technical and inspirational knowledge—even though we didn't retain the knowledge of our origins."

"With Wankatanka's guidance, we welcomed the descendants of the Atlantians into our South Dakota community," Zeke added.

"What you are saying," Alicia said, "is that you two, Stephanie and Zeke, are descendants of both the Olympians and the muses—your Wankatanka?"

"She prefers the name: *Benta,*" Zeke said.

"Benta," Otto mused. "Isn't that the name of the structural tube we walked through."

"We had to honor her in some way for the inspiration," Zeke said.

CHAPTER 11

That evening, Cheryl and Pythia were seated in the Red Lounge enjoying an after-dinner glass of wine.

"So, my friend, what was it like being an Olympian and living in nine-dimensional space?" Cheryl asked.

Pythia blushed. "I was never an Olympian," she corrected.

Cheryl blinked, and asked, "I thought you said that you were Apollo's high priestess."

"Apollo is the Olympian. I was only a commoner who was linked to him through thought. He would proclaim vague prophecies through me. Prophecies that aided farmers in their crop planting or warned of wars with other city-states."

"Vague prophecies? That is odd. The prophesy he sent you about our Martian Colony's destruction was not vague at all. He appeared to you with a warning. A warning that

205

materialized from the dream world into our world. If it were not for that magnificent piece of parchment that he gave you, we would now be ashes on the Martian surface," Cheryl stated.

Pythia sipped her wine and nodded in agreement. While seated next to the lounge's window she stared at the stars that whizzed by.

"I guess," Cheryl continued, "because of the evolutionary event that took place in some regions of the universe that transformed Apollo from a nine-dimensional being to a ten-dimensional one, he was able to hone his thought processes."

Pythia considered this explanation.

Cheryl sipped wine from her glass, and said, "tell me more about this evolutionary process—about this *Clarity.*

Pythia perked up, stared into Cheryl's eyes, and said, "I don't know much about it, but I can somewhat recite what I learned when I lived on Delphi. Are you familiar with bible studies on Earth?"

Being born into the Catholic faith as well as enduring years of religious instruction as a child, Cheryl nodded, and said, "oh yes. I am very familiar with bible studies."

"Well, in the *Book of Genesis*, God created the Heavens and the Earth. The Earth was a formless wasteland and darkness covered the abyss and a mighty wind swept over the water."

"I didn't mean that you had to go back to the history of everything," Cheryl smirked as she gulped the remaining wine in her glass.

Seeing that she was almost done with her wine also, Pythia took both glasses, stood up, and said, "indulge me. First, I will get us another glass of wine."

Cheryl initially watched her friend walk to the bar, then she turned her attention towards the star-filled window. Never in her wildest dreams would she have imagined herself amongst these heavens.

"Okay," Pythia said as she placed a glass of wine in front of Cheryl, and continued, "when God saw the vast wasteland covered in darkness before him, guess what he said next?"

Remembering her *Catechism*, Cheryl spouted, "let there be light."

With those words the two women silently sipped their wine while pensively staring at the window of zooming stars.

In earlier days when Cheryl became a scientist, she exchanged this *Genesis* story for the *Big Bang Theory* which, in essence, stated the same philosophy—that something came from nothing; only, the *Big Bang* did not have a higher being creating the *something*.

"The Olympians," Pythia continued, "believed that instead of a universe filled with darkness; it was filled with *Chaos*."

"That sounds ominous," Cheryl said.

"Indeed," Pythia agreed. "It was an abyss of darkness, confusion, fear. *Chaos* preceded the light."

"And *Clarity*?" Cheryl asked, "is it that light? The light of consciousness?"

Pythia nodded.

"So, let me get this straight," Cheryl said as if cramming for a college examination. "So, Thia—the goddess of all gods—is part Olympian and part muse. Muses live in the abstract. Or another way to put it, in a world of energy and thought. Thia's mother, Dione, who is a muse, knew that *Chaos* was going to, once again, overtake the universe and extinguish humanity's light. And she also knew that *Clarity*, or the light, was battling *Chaos* for dominance. So, with the aid of the South Dakota community—mainly Thia—they brightened two beacons of light across the universe. These beacons lit the way for *Clarity* to establish a foothold which kept *Chaos* at bay."

"Very good," Pythia complimented her friend. "I never thought that a hardcore scientist such as yourself could grasp such a concept."

Cheryl looked drained. She closed her eyes and began to massage her temples. When she opened her eyes, she was shocked to see Apollo standing near their table.

"May I join you ladies?" Apollo asked.

Pythia smiled broadly, nodded at the chair next to her, and said, "please do."

No longer frightened of Apollo after they shared the black-hole experience where she saw Apollo's true self, Cheryl's scientific mind kicked in, and she said, "I have a few questions that maybe you can answer."

Remembering Cheryl's indigo glow during the black-hole experience and how he wanted to get to know her further,

Apollo welcomed the chance to talk with her, and said, "if I don't have the answers to your questions, I will try my best to find out. Fire away!"

"Well, my first question is: when you move through three-dimensional time, do you have access to everyone's past, present, and future?"

Pleased at such a thoughtful question, Apollo answered, "I am moving through my *own* past, present, and future."

"Then, how did you know about the imminent destruction of our Martian colony?"

Except for his sister, Thia, most beings accepted Apollo's actions unconditionally. Few beings—even other Olympians—questioned him. Even though all Olympians had an ability to move through time, they were lazy. Moving through time took practice and persistence; two qualities that Apollo possessed.

Apollo silently sipped from his wine glass. Seeing that Cheryl required no god-like gestures, he simply winked at her, and replied, "it was lucky for you that my dear, Pythia, resided at your colony. When I moved through time and noted that Pythia was no longer part of my future, I alerted my sister."

Cheryl saw the pride that welled up within Pythia when Apollo mentioned their relationship.

Apollo faced Pythia, held her hand, and continued, "Pythia has always been a part of my past, present, and future. And when my future existed without her, I became concerned."

"But you hadn't seen Pythia since you were a young boy on Delphi. Is that correct?" Cheryl asked.

Apollo nodded. "That's absolutely right. Although I had not physically seen her for thousands of Earth years, I always felt her near me."

Looking into Apollo's loving eyes, Pythia sighed with happiness.

"Okay," Cheryl continued, "so when you alerted Thia, what happened next?"

"Next," Apollo answered, "Thia searched her own space-time dimensions and confirmed that Pythia was no longer part of our futures. After she confirmed this, Thia alerted her husband, Stash. Stash—who is also an Olympian and was exiled to Earth with Thia and Pythia—also had the ability to search time. When Stash searched his space-time dimensions, he found that a family member of his—from his last reincarnation—also wasn't part of his future."

Cheryl was silent for a few moments, then asked, "were they all erased at the same time?"

Apollo turned his attention from Pythia to Cheryl. He was amazed with her questioning. Usually, most people could not engage him in a conversation on this level, let along, progress the conversation further. He nodded, and confirmed, "they were erased at the same time. A time after the Earth-Moon disaster."

"So, with three points of time fixed, you were able to triangulate where we were in space," Cheryl hypothesized.

"What?" Pythia asked her friend.

"Triangulation is a surveying technique. It is a method used when people are looking for something, but just can't get an accurate location," Cheryl said.

"Apollo nodded, and said, "That is exactly right. It took three of us to locate your exact location in Space. Through a time-and-space triangulation, we were able to pinpoint the exact time and location that Pythia was erased from our futures."

Cheryl absorbed this, then said, "that solves that mystery. You used basic science; yet, at a higher level. Now my next question has to do with the evolutionary process. Pythia was just explaining the evolutionary event that took place recently in the universe. My question is: how long will it take for us Martian colonists get to that evolutionary stage? Will it be twenty generations from now?"

Apollo winked at Cheryl, and answered, "not necessarily."

"What do you mean? Like you so graciously explained at dinner, we are four-dimensional creatures. We are three-dimensional people who step through time on a linear basis."

"Of course, you are," Apollo agreed. "However, *Clarity* is here. And I can help you both to achieve ten-dimensions status within a week at most."

CHAPTER 12

Over the next seven days, Thia, Apollo, and Zeke Hawkfeather held enlightenment practices throughout the spaceship for those who wanted the knowledge. Each of the practices were held in one of the three forests located throughout the vessel. These locations were necessary for both their calming effect and connection with nature. The forests contained: a horizon-to-horizon view of space—filled with blackness and dotted with bright, intermittent stars and massive, colorful, stellar-nursery gas clouds; a river complete with the soothing sound of flowing water; and a plethora of forest, non-human life such as trees, grasses, birds, and insects.

On the fifth day of these practice sessions, Cheryl sat next to Pythia while preparing herself for the next session. These practices were learned in a series of progressions. Each day building upon the previous days. The first day, Cheryl

212

learned how to sit properly. Proper posture was necessary so that her body could release most of its tension; leaving only the tension necessary in the muscles to support her body in an upright, sitting position. The second day, she learned how to breathe properly. With the accompaniment of correct posture, enhanced breathing was meant to lengthen life. She learned that breathing was not only a physical act, but it was also an act of receiving that vigilance energy—or life force—from the universe. The third day, she learned relaxation. She learned that relaxation allows the body to replenish its energy reserves in preparation of the next day's activity. The fourth day, she learned meditation. She learned how to envision her body, mind, and the universal consciousness.

As Cheryl calmed her body and mind while practicing proper posture, breathing, relaxation, and meditation; she heard Apollo's voice when he spoke to his group of two-hundred individuals that were scattered throughout the forest.

"I am proud of each one of you. You have trained your minds to focus; to be present. Today, we will practice moving through our past, present, and future. Today we will try to exist in the three-dimensional world of time."

Feeling that her calm heartbeat began to quicken, Cheryl took deep, slow breaths. Then after her heart settled back into a slow, rhythmic beat, she focused her mind on her past. This was extremely difficult for her. Whenever she consciously thought of the past, she became frightened. Her past was clouded with her husband's death. Since his death, she subconsciously lingered in the past. Whenever she was not

213

working or enjoying Fly's company, she grievously thought of her dead husband. Cheryl thought of the agony he must have endured just before dying. These thoughts always brought her sorrow. They overshadowed everything she did in the present. Preceding her husband's untimely death, Cheryl was the consummate optimist. She always made plans for a hopeful future. However, since she lived with the devastating events of the past, she feared the future. She feared not only for herself, but for Fly. This crippling fear kept her from hopeful thoughts.

During the previous days' lessons, Apollo imparted his philosophy on the group. He encouraged them to find bright spots in their timelines and avoid the dark spots. The bright spots, if sought out thoroughly, would outshine the dark spots. Apollo named the bright spots, *Clarity*, and the dark spots, *Chaos*. He insisted that after these spots were given names, then they can be lived with or defeated.

Remembering those words, Cheryl named her husband's death: Chaos. Once named, she pushed her thoughts past that hurtful time. Doing so, allowed her to see the past clearly. She saw her childhood. She remembered how happy she was as a child. She saw the day she got married. She saw the love in her husband's eyes when he affirmed his wedding vows to her. She saw the day she gave birth to Fly. That was the happiest day of her life! And she saw all the happy times she enjoyed with Fly and her husband. After seeing all the joys from her past life, she no longer feared it. With fear gone, her mind was, once again, opened to a future filled with hope.

On the sixth day of the practice session, Cheryl learned to focus her attention on universal thought. During his pre-session lecture, Apollo reminded everyone that all matter is made of atoms which contained such particles as neutrons, protons and, most importantly, electrons. He instructed everyone to hold a piece of matter in their hands. Whether the substance was a blade of grass, a rock, or a leaf on the trees. Next, he encouraged his group to visualize the neurons that traveled from their brains and flowed through their parasympathetic nervous system. He told them that these neurons were messengers from the brain—in the form of electrical impulses—to their internal organs during rest. Finally, he told them to visualize their electrical impulses interacting with the electrons of the external object they connected with.

Cheryl, following Apollo's instructions, sat in a meditative state while visualizing the flow of energy from her body to the rock that she held in her hand. In this state, time had no meaning; only energy existed. She felt energy flow through her body like a fresh stream of water. It flowed from her brain, through her hand and into the rock. Once the energy flowed into the rock, the object became part of her. Her energy and the energy within the rock were the same; there were no boundaries.

Cheryl sat in this position and state of mind until her body began to ache. Aware of her soar and tired joints, she opened her eyes. When Cheryl opened her eyes, she saw that Apollo was the only person that remained in the forest.

"Oh my," Cheryl said, "how long have I been sitting here?"

Apollo smiled while reaching down to help her stand up, and answered, "just about twelve hours."

Cheryl grabbed his hand and stood up. Upon standing, she stretched her neck from side to side, and said, "I am going back to my apartment for a long, hot bath."

CHAPTER 13

Zeke Hawkfeather also educated a group of two-hundred colonists in the ways of enlightenment. The grandson of a Sioux Indian holy-man, Zeke found his true nature when he embarked on his *vision quest* in the Black Hills of South Dakota. During his *vision quest*, he communicated with nature and found a connection with the spirit world where he gained strength and wisdom.

Fly, Otto, Alicia, Gregory, and Heather sat in Zeke's class. The five teens sat on the forest floor of the recreational orb. Fly had a head start on his path to enlightenment. Earlier in life, he connected with the musical world. Through his written and instrumental creativity, his mind was open to possibilities.

On the last day, once Fly achieved a meditative state, he began to connect with the natural world. After Zeke instructed

217

everyone to find something in the forest to connect with, Fly found a mushroom. As he tenderly touched the mushroom while in a deep meditative state, the energy that flowed through his parasympathetic nervous system connected with the mushroom's energy. The mushroom, part of the forest's vast *mycelium network*, connected with plant life throughout the forest. The Mycelium Network—an electrochemical, microscopic web—connects the forest's organisms on a subsurface level. By embracing the mushroom in his meditative state, Fly's electrochemical makeup became part of the vast forest network. In this state, he not only connected with the mushroom, but he also connected with every tree in the forest. His molecules were interacting with other molecules; not just the trees, but the birds that flew in the trees as well as the insects that crawled through the soil.

After their last session, Fly, Otto, Alicia, Gregory, and Heather invited Zeke, Pulo, and Stephanie to join them for a beer at the lounge.

"So," began Fly as he held his glass of beer up to the light and examined the amber liquid, "as a tenth-dimensional being, I won't need food for nourishment?"

Zeke nodded, and answered, "that is correct. You can get your energy from interacting with your surroundings."

"That's right," Stephanie added, "when your molecules interact with other molecules, you exchange energy. We don't really have to eat."

218

"What about me?" Otto asked, "I haven't achieved the tenth-dimension status. When we get to Zenti, how will I be nourished?"

Stephanie smiled at Otto, and replied, "our Zentian community is composed of over ten-thousand people. And, although most chose enlightenment, others have not. If you choose to continue with your teachings, you can become ten-dimensional. I can provide you with personal lessons if you like. I sense that you are almost there."

"I have a question," Gregory eagerly said. "When I am in a molecular state, am I invisible?"

Zeke nodded, and replied, "in that molecular stage, you are invisible to the naked eye."

"If we are invisible," Alicia interrupted, "when we become visible, can we rearrange our molecules into something else—like a butterfly?"

Zeke winked at Alicia, and answered, "absolutely! Transformation is the fun part."

"You mean," said Heather, "I can change myself into a beauty queen?"

Stephanie laughed, and replied, "sure, you can do that. But it takes an enormous amount of energy to hold that form for very long."

"What about death?" Alicia asked. "When I explored my three-dimensional timeline, didn't see my death."

"That is the awesome part," Pulo chimed in. "Because we have the ability to reduce ourselves to a molecular level and our cells are made up of molecules; we have the ability to repair our cells before they degrade."

"You mean that our cells never age?" Alicia concluded.

Pulo nodded, and said, "only if you want them to age. If you repair them, you can live forever provided you don't have a life-threating accident."

While listening to this line of conversation, Otto decided to take Stephanie up on her offer to become ten-dimensional.

The teens silently drank their beers while exploring all the possibilities of their new world.

While thinking, Gregory's eyes wondered towards a table where Thia and Apollo sat in lively conversation. He noticed that both Thia and Pulo looked related. They had the same dark-brown skin and the same tight, curly hair. However, the rumors he heard about their relationship had to be false. Since Pulo was sitting with them, he asked, "what is your relationship with Thia?"

Knowing this was a complicated relationship, Pulo leaned back in his chair, gulped a large portion of beer, and answered, "she is my grandmother."

Heather eyed Thia from head to toe, and said, "there is no way that woman is your grandmother. Why, she is in her mid-twenties!"

Pulo smiled, and explained, "there are a few factors that must come into my answer. First, humans on Delphi age slower than humans from Earth. For example, I am four-thousands of your earth-years old."

220

Everyone who sat around the table—except for Zeke and Stephanie—silently gasped.

"You have all heard the story of Thia's exile from Delphi and her subsequent reincarnations on Earth?"

The teens silently nodded in unison.

"Well," Pulo continued, "at that time, my grandfather, Ptolemy, was also exiled. And at the time of his banishment, my mother—his daughter—was only three years old. My mother raised me with the help of Apollo."

"And, while exiled on Earth, both Ptolemy and Thia endured thousands of years of reincarnations. And, through all of that, they still found one another. They truly loved each other. These two, old souls, found each other one final time, and moved to the South Dakota community."

Looking at the table where Thia and Apollo were talking and laughing, Alicia commented, "how romantic."

"Of course, when Ptolemy returned to Delphi, he looked nothing like the grandfather my mother told me about. The Ptolemy of Delphi was over six-feet tall with broad, muscular shoulders. He was a demigod born from Zeus' son Ares and a village woman. His skin was as black as ebony and his hair was as tightly curled as mine," Pulo said as he rubbed his hands over the thick, brown coils. "Grandfather, Ptolemy, or Stash, as he now is called is married to Thia. That union makes Thia my grandmother," Pulo concluded.

"Stash, who is also my cousin," Stephanie added, is Ptolemy reincarnated. He stands under six-feet tall. His hair is

221

thickly blond, and his eyes are bright green. He comes from a long line of German military officers and politicians."

Zeke laughed when noticing the blank stares on the other teen's faces. "Stephanie's cousin, Stash, and Ptolemy are the same person. Although they possess different-looking bodies, their souls are the same."

Otto scratched his head, and asked, "so, Stephanie's cousin, who is both Thia's husband and Pulo's grandfather, is Ptolemy?"

"You got it," Zeke said. "You will all meet Stash when we arrive at Zenti. And, although he does not claim to be, he is the unofficial head of our Zentians colony."

CHAPTER 14

As the galaxy-class starship blasted through the universe at an inconceivable speed of millions of light-years-per-day, Cheryl stood at her favorite window in the Red Lounge and stared ahead at their new home. Although they were surrounded by stars, ahead of them stood a bright ball of massive stars tightly clustered together.

"That's the Sombrero Galaxy," said Fly who materialized next to her.

Cheryl was so absorbed in thought while focused on the upcoming galaxy, she startled at the sudden appearance of her son.

Fly handed Cheryl a glass of red wine while he stood next to her, and said, "isn't that amazing, Mom?"

Cheryl took the wine from her son. She smiled while looking into those familiar warm, brown eyes. She immediately recognized a difference in Fly. Both she and Fly were very busy since they boarded the starship. They not only lived in different apartments, but they also practiced enlightenment sessions in different groups. So, seeing a sharp change in her son was clear. She saw that he grieved no more for his father. She saw that his spirit was happier and lighter just like when he was a child. And looking deeper into those rich, happy eyes of his, she saw, as well as felt, that he had achieved the status of a ten-dimensional being.

Fly noticed the same about his mother. After his father's death, he noticed that a part of his mother also died. And, although she was still kind and sweet, she was not happy. Now, he felt the return of her joyfulness. Without speaking a word, he knew that his mother was on her way to becoming a ten-dimensional being. He saw that the part of her that died with his father was returned. He reasoned that they both recognized that his father was not lost to them but was a part of them, living in them.

They watched in silence as they approached the galaxy. True to its name, the galaxy looked like a massive Sombrero. This lens-shaped galaxy contained billions of stars sprawled over thirty-one light-years. The Sombrero Galaxy boasted two prominent features. First, a dark, thick dust-ring surrounded the galaxy that looked like the brim of a sombrero; hence, its name. This symmetrical ring, which enclosed the galaxy's center bulge, was composed of cold, atomic, hydrogen gas, and dust. And second, in the center of the galaxy sat a mega-watt, super-massive, black hole.

Because of the galaxy's brightness, the Red Lounge's ambient lighting began to increase gradually just like a rising sun would increase light from morning to noon.

Cheryl held up her glass of wine, and said, "cheers to our new home!"

Fly touched Cheryl's glass with his mug of beer making a clinking sound, and said, "to our new home."

When Pythia appeared at Cheryl's side with a wide grin and a goblet of wine, she said to Fly, "Alicia is looking for you."

Cheryl and Pythia watched Fly as he sought out his friends. The two women stood next to each other all smiles. Pythia was amazed by not only the view outside the window, but the festive nature of everyone. People drank, danced, and engaged in loud conversations. She could hardly believe that only two weeks previous this group was saddened, demoralized, and frightened. Only two weeks ago, they watched as their only home was destroyed within hours. And, as they watched, they could not visualize a future. Now, their future was outside this starship's window.

Within minutes, the ship entered the Sombrero Galaxy. Upon entering, the ambient lighting onboard grew even brighter. And, as the light brightened, Pythia found that their circle of two increased to three. Apollo joined the two women.

Cheryl, no longer afraid of Apollo, smiled broadly at him, and said, "I am unsure if anyone has thanked you. If not,

225

thank you for saving all of us and bringing us to a bright, new home."

PART III

The Age of Aquarius

A Force for Clarity

CHAPTER 1

Look over there! Look at that!" Heather shrieked as she pointed to a bright spot on the planet.

Following the direction where Heather pointed, Otto, Alicia, Fly, and Gregory saw a white blob located on the side of the mountain chain that came into view. As the spaceship entered the planet's atmosphere and descended to within two miles of its surface, not only could the ship's inhabitants see lush trees, flowing streams, massive mountain formations complete with thick, green forests; but they also got a clearer view of the bright spot. It was their new home.

Situated on the side of mountain and overlooking an aquamarine ocean, sat a catacomb of white structures trimmed in blue. As the spaceship effortlessly landed like a soft feather, its inhabitants were overwhelmed with the outside view.

"Hello everyone," Thia said over the intercom, "outside, is your new home. I know that almost all of you entered this ship with only the cloths on your backs. Therefore, whatever cloths you found in your shipboard apartments are

228

yours to take if you wish. Soon, we will be disembarking. Upon leaving this starship, everyone will have apartment assignments in the new-earth city. And, as you can see, we landed just a half-mile away from the city. So, gather what you want to take and meet at the exit door. Oh, and welcome home!"

At the conclusion Thia's announcement, Heather grabbed Alicia's hand, and said, "a new home! Let us explore."

Together, Heather and Alicia stepped out of the spaceship's large, hangar door. On their heels, were Otto, Fly, and Gregory. Once outside the ship, Heather let go of Alicia's hand and spun around under the warm sunlight. Simultaneously, as Heather let go of Alicia's hand, Gregory softly laced fingers with hers.

"So far, this is like our dreams," Gregory said while looking into Alicia's eyes.

Alicia nodded. Just like her dream, she felt the warmth of the sun on her cheeks, she felt blades of grass soften her walk, and she inhaled clean, warm air.

Alicia smiled broadly while *feeling* their new environment. After living on the Martian surface, while confined to the artificial environment of the bio-domes, she luxuriated in breathing fresh air and feeling the warmth of a real sun on her skin. While still holding Gregory's hand, she looked into his smiling eyes, and asked, "shall we continue on our journey and explore our new home?"

The spaceship landed adjacent to the community of homes, therefore, the group had only a twenty-minute walk. With the ocean to their backs, they walked up a small slope that led to a broad, wide, grass-filled plateau. Lined with Grecian columns, this lush plateau contained many gardens and

229

pathways that led to the abundance of honeycombed, white, and blue-trimmed apartments.

After they walked through the garden, they came to a large, marble-tiled square. This one-mile square—also lined with marble columns and planters sprouting green ferns and colorful flowers—sat in front of the domiciles. After passing the square, they, once again, came to a twenty-foot-wide walkway. Covered with a lattice and lined with columns, this walkway was spacious. Ferns and flowers hung from the overhead lattice. This half-mile-long walkway ended perpendicular to a mile-long hallway. On one side of the hallway was a clear-glass window with a view of the square, and on the other side was a honeycomb of over one-thousand doorways. Each doorway was numbered.

Looking at the numbers displayed over the doorways, Alicia saw a similar pattern. Like the layout of the starship, these apartments were designed with wide hallways that were lined with apartment doorways. Before she said anything, Heather was, once again, at her side.

"Hey, I got our room assignment," Heather said to Alicia.

Alicia smiled, let go of Gregory's hand, and said, "I think you should find who you are bunking with." Then turning to Heather, she said, "let's go!"

After Gregory departed, Alicia and Heather walked only a few steps to a door that displayed their range of numbers. Walking through the door, they encountered a stairway, which was also an escalator. The escalator stretched one-hundred-and-fifty feet from bottom to top. Riding on the escalator, Alicia and Heather passed doors with numbers that were within the range of their apartment. When they reached the very top, they came to their door.

Looking at their apartment number and seeing that the doors had no knobs to assist with opening, Alicia concluded that these doors worked like the ones on the spaceship, so she said, "open please."

With those simple words, the door slid into a wall. They peeped through the opening and saw their apartment. When Alicia and Heather stepped over the threshold, they both were astounded at what they saw. Although the apartment was like the abode they occupied on the starship, the wall opposite the door was made of clear glass with a clear-glass door in its center.

Heather ran to the door. Upon her approach, the door automatically slid open. She crossed the threshold and stepped out to a large, tiled deck. And, since they were on the top floor, they had a full view of the walkway, courtyard, grassy area, and ocean. "This is magnificent!" Heather said while leaning on the deck's railing and breathing in the cool, ocean breeze. This apartment reminded her of her family's summer home in Greece. "I could actually just live on this deck." Built into a sloping mountain, all the domiciles' decks, like theirs, had a view of the sky.

Alicia also noted that the deck was fully furnished. It contained deck chairs and a breakfast table with accompanying chairs. "Can you believe that this deck is completely private, the only views are the sky above and the ocean below; we can't see any neighbors," Alicia said. "Let's go explore the rest of our home."

Like the apartment on the starship, this residence was about two-thousand square feet with two bedrooms, a large bathroom, and a combined kitchen and dining room. Also, like the apartment on the starship, this apartment came with a fully stocked kitchen. To their surprise, there were plates, pots,

231

pans, flatware, drinking glasses, and every type of serving spoon and cutlery imaginable. All the furniture was dark wood. The sofa and other chairs were a dark-brown leather. The walls were artfully painted. Two of the four walls in each room were a salmon pink, a third wall was panted rust, and the fourth wall was all glass: providing a view of the ocean. Moreover, salmon pink and rust, porcelain tile covered every square inch of the floor.

"Look here," said Alicia while sitting on the sofa, which was facing the windowed wall that opened out to the deck.

Heather sat next to Alicia who held a booklet in her hands.

"This booklet tells us everything about the apartment. It is a users' manual," Alicia excitedly said while fingering each page. "Look here," she pointed at the page where a box with a clear, small door was displayed, and asked, "where is it?"

Energetically, Heather stood up and pointed at a two-foot-squared, clear door that was located next to the refrigerator, and said, "over there."

The two women quickly walked to the door, and then with a smile on her face, Alicia said, "I would like a glass of white wine please."

Within seconds, they saw a glass of wine materialize behind the glass.

Cautiously, Alicia opened the door, removed the white wine, tasted it, and said, "this has many possibilities!"

This new prospect excited Heather, so she squealed, "my turn. I want to take a turn." Then looking at the door, she said, "I would like a glass of red wine please."

Similarly, a glass of red wine appeared.

"This is totally awesome," Heather said after reaching for the glass and sipping it.

After the two returned with their drinks and sat on the sofa, Alicia said, "according to this users' manual we can program our favorite recipes into this technological wonder and request any meal we wish.

Before, Heather could not have imagined such technology. She thought of the options, and said aloud, "I wonder if there is something similar for creating cloths?"

Hearing Heather's musing, Alicia flipped through the manual, and said, "eureka! Here it is. There is a similar device near the bedroom where we can materialize clothing and any other object that is programmed into it." Alicia's eyes sparkled even more when he turned the page and spotted another technological marvel. "And look at this!" She exclaimed. "Next to the cloths box is another one that you can clean anything—it needs no water—it is a *sonic* cleaner!"

After viewing and using these devices, the two exhaustedly fell to the sofa.

"How about we enjoy our wine on the deck?" Heather suggested.

"Great Idea," Alicia agreed.

The two women carried their glasses to the deck. There, they lounged in cushioned chairs as they stared at the dynamic ocean capped with silver waves. However, before they completely absorbed their surroundings, a voice sounded.

"There are visitors at your door," came a computer-generated, woman's voice.

At that announcement, the women giddily looked at each other.

"What do we do?" Heather asked.

Alicia shrugged her shoulders, and replied, "answer it—
I suppose."

Heather popped up from her seat, ran excitedly to the
door, and hesitantly said, "come in?"

At her request, the door disintegrated revealing Fly,
Otto, and Gregory standing in the hallway.

Heather flew to Fly and excitedly hugged him.

Grinning at Heather's enthusiasm, Alicia said to the
guys, "come in. We were just having some drinks on the
deck."

As the sun slipped beneath the ocean's horizon, leaving
a semi-lighted sky; the five teenagers silently sat on the
balcony watching the silver waves play across the ocean's face.
In their silence, they were nearly startled when the apartment's
voice announced visitors at the door.

Alicia, with wine glass in hand, walked to the door, and
said, "come in, please."

The apartment's entrance disintegrated. In its place,
Alicia saw Zeke, Stephanie, and Pulo standing at the entrance.

First to enter, Stephanie handed Alicia a bouquet of
flowers, and said, "welcome to your new home."

All smiles, Alicia took the flowers, hugged all three,
and said, "everyone is on the balcony. Hey, get yourselves
drinks and join us outside." Then marveling at the fragrant
flowers, she added, "I will put these in water then join you guys
out there."

As soon as everyone was gathered on the balcony, Zeke
said, "in a few days, we will embark on a mission for *Clarity,*
and we were hopeful that you guys join us."

Knowing that they were not nearly as advanced as the
Zentians, Otto asked, "how can we help *you*?"

234

"We have a briefing tomorrow afternoon at three o'clock. You can find out more then."

CHAPTER 2

The next morning, Alicia, and Heather enjoyed an energizing cup of coffee while sitting on their oceanfront balcony. Upon finishing their coffees, they exited their apartment, walked for twenty minutes, and arrived at the community center. This center sat apart from the apartment buildings. Like on the starship, there were gyms, cafeterias, and meeting rooms. When the two women entered a small auditorium, they found their friends and sat next to them.

The auditorium's seating capacity topped out at sixty people. The tiered structure culminated at a stage located on its lowest level. Sitting in one of the top-tier seats, Alicia saw that the room was only one-third full. She also noticed that the stage—at the bottom level—was populated with seven individuals who all sat behind a dais.

Alicia recognized five of the seven people that populated the dais: Stephanie, Zeke, Thia, Doctor Beckman, and Apollo. Thia was immediately flanked by two men; one was German-looking and the other was Native-American looking. Although the German-looking man who sat on Thia's right was alien to Alicia, the sight of the Native-American looking man, who sat on Thia's left, quickened her heart. This was the man from her dreams. In her dream there was a worm that crawled on her hand. This worm then turned into a man. This was the man she thought was her grandfather. Understandingly, however, it was not her grandfather, it was the man on the stage who sat next to Thia!

Thia, who sat in the middle of the dais rose from her seat, looked over the crowd, and said, "I would like to welcome you all here. I want to, particularly, welcome our new members from the Martian settlement."

With those words, the Zentians applauded the former, Martian colonists.

"Now," Thia continued, "before we begin this briefing, I would like to introduce the former colonists to two of our council members. To my right is my husband, Stash, who directs most of our missions. And to my left is my mentor, Worm, who helps us communicate with *Clarity*."

'So, it was him,' Alicia thought to herself. 'He was the worm!' She said while examining the Native-American elder. And, knowing that he communicated directly with her across galaxies, Alicia wanted to become acquainted with this man.

"At this point," Thia continued, "I will turn the briefing over to Stash."

Otto sized Stash up. Otto saw a slender man, in his early thirties, under six-feet tall, with Germanic features, and a crop of thick, chin-length, blond hair that was parted down the middle of his head and tucked neatly behind both ears.

"This man is an Olympian?" Otto whispered to Fly, who sat next to him. "He used to be tall, black-skinned, and muscular? And *he* is Pulo's grandfather?"

Fly shrugged his shoulders, and replied, "I guess this is what happens after thousands of years of reincarnations."

Without any introductory words, Stash got to the point. "Our community was gifted the mission to bring *Clarity* to the universe. And we accomplish this mission by first, selecting emerging worlds; second, enlightening them; and third, having them spread that enlightenment."

Eager to understand the mission, Fly raised his hand.

Seeing the young man's raised hand, Stash asked, "Fly, is it?"

Fly's eyes widened in surprise that the community's leader knew his name. Collecting himself, he said, "yes, sir. My name is Fly. What is an *emerging* world?"

Stash smiled, broadened his focus to the entire audience, and said, "my apologies. I forget how much everyone knows about our mission. Please feel free to ask any question at any time." Then looking directly at Fly, he continued, "back to this young man's question. An emerging world is one where most of its inhabitants are on the verge of evolving into ten-dimensional beings. Furthermore, on this world, some individuals have already evolved. We identify and infiltrate the world to learn more about them to see if they are truly capable of evolution. We have identified one such world. And, although this world is on the brink of evolving, it is also on the brink of extinction. This world has several, desperate kingdoms that maintain their power through might and fear. They use might to keep the other kingdoms at bay and they use fear to control their populations."

"That sounds like Earth's old, political structure," Gregory whispered to Alicia.

Alicia nodded in agreement.

238

"Upon infiltrating this spacefaring world," Stash continued, "we identified the kingdom with the best chance to lead their entire world to enlightenment. Representatives from that kingdom have already landed on Zenti. They are here under a ruse that there is a special artifact located on Zenti that will bestow ultimate power to them; thus, allowing them to conquer the other kingdoms on their planet."

Alicia raised her hand.

"Yes, Alicia," Stash said. "Do you have a question?"

"So, you are going to trick them into enlightenment? From all the training we received on your starship to become ten-dimensional beings, I thought an individual had to open their own mind to enlightenment and want it!"

"You are absolutely right, young lady," Stash responded. "We cannot trick anyone into enlightenment. They must want to evolve. However, we can show them a path to enlightenment and hope they will follow that course. So, that's why we asked you—the newly enlightened—to help us show them that path."

CHAPTER 3

Upon landing on Zenti, thirty of the spaceship's forty inhabitants exited the vehicle. Led by their prince—a tall, broad-shouldered, young man in his early twenties—the expedition headed towards a steep mountain range located to the east.

Struggling to keep up with the group, the prince's servant, Speke, carried more than his sleeping roll. He also dragged behind him food provisions for the evening's meal on a hover-pallet. Even though he struggled, Speke was not hindered by his burdens; he only marveled at the tall trees bursting with flowers the colors he had never seen before. He loved the natural world that this planet offered. Unlike his industrialized planet complete with unsafe, polluted air and water which irritated the very senses; this planet had a calming effect on his soul.

"What a lovely planet," Speke said as he caught up with his master.

Arrogantly, the prince looked ahead at the mountain while ignoring the clear brook he trampled through as well as the aromas emitted from the fragrant flowers.

"Yes," he replied, "after we retrieve the artifact, we can conquer this planet also."

Even though Speke and his master liked the planet for different reasons, he knew that the prince's intentions were noble. He knew that his prince wanted only good for his people. Speke also knew that their world would survive if all the people were united and treated fairly. Presently, on his world, a minority of people in all kingdoms were hunted down and put to death. The hunted were persecuted because they developed *new ways*. Their *new ways* included: mind-reading, levitation, telekinesis, and invisibility. Fearful of these individuals—afraid they would take power and upend the status quo—most kingdoms eliminated them. The individuals that were not captured and killed became members of a secret, underground movement.

Speke, on the other hand, did not develop the *new ways*, he was born with them—he was born from *Clarity*—making him the most powerful of these individuals. Being born from *Clarity*, Speke was able to live in his past, present, and future. He saw that his future was filled with destruction. He saw that, if left unchecked, the leaders of his planet would destroy everyone in their quest for power. Intuitively, he knew that if people with *new ways* were integrated into their society, then they would eventually upset the balance of power and sway the powerful people to embrace the light. Moreover, he knew that of all the noble families on his planet, this prince, though arrogant, had the compassion to unite everyone—even those gifted with *new ways*— and save their world. So, instead of going into hiding by joining an underground movement, Speke decided to tackle his oppressors by changing the minds of the most powerful ones. And even though he had the ability to strike down anyone who dared to harm him—like his master— he pretended to be a bumbling, idiot servant.

Speke walked side-by-side with his master until his master's uncle—who also held the position as *commander of all generals*—pushed his way between the two.

"My prince, might I make a suggestion," said General Toland.

With squared shoulders and eyes trained ahead on the mountain range, Prince Xant commanded, "you may speak, uncle."

"Since this is unfamiliar terrain and it may be another day before we reach our destination, I suggest that we pitch our tents and make camp within the hour before night falls."

The prince stopped walking and looked back at the men that accompanied him. Seeing that most of them dragged hover-pallets filled with tents, sleeping provisions, and weapons; he considered the suggestion. Though he was eager to obtain the artifact and be on his way, he did not want to exhaust his men. The prince looked passed the stand of fragrant trees, beyond the meadow that laid ahead, and towards the looming, heavily-wooded mountain-range, and said, "very well, uncle. It should take us a couple of hours to cross that meadow which will land us at the foot of the mountain range. We can make camp there."

Within two hours, the expedition emerged from the stand of flowering trees, reached the meadow near the foot of the mountain range, and made camp. Unlike most of the soldiers, Speke did not pitch a tent. Because he served the prince, he usually slept on a mat in the corner of the prince's tent. However, like the soldiers, he did have duties to perform once they reached the meadow. The main duty involved gathering wood for the fire he needed to cook the troop's evening meal. After procuring wood, he set up a tripod over the tent of wood then he secured a cast-iron pot to a hook that hang from the apex of the tripod. While water boiled in the massive kettle, Speke sliced and diced vegetables and meats which he added to the boiling water. After seasoning the meal with special herbs and spices, he allowed it to cook while he unpacked other dinner provisions such as hearty breads, bottles of wine, and eating utensils.

While setting up a serving table, Speke hummed a song. Humming was a way to center himself. Although he knew that he did not have to do these manual tasks—that he could use his *new-ways* gifts to accomplish them in a fraction of the time— he forced himself to see the larger picture. A picture in which someday he could freely be himself. He knew of people with *new ways* who used their gifts at all costs. He knew too many people who were put to death because they were empowered by their gifts. These people arrogantly saw themselves better than the others.

As the sun silkily slipped beneath the mountain tops, evening campfires popped up throughout the campsite which was filled with at least ten gleaming, white, rectangular, cloth tents. And, as always, once these fires burned, the soldiers gathered around Speke's serving table. Noticing that the prince's uncle was already drinking wine and eating a chunk of bread, the rest of the men joined in.

"Dinner is ready," Speke said to the men as they lingered around the kettle.

After the prince and his uncle were served, one-by-one each man ladled venison stew from the large, cast-iron kettle into tin bowls. While eating and drinking, voices began to rise.

In their usual joviality, some men taunted others while some broke into song. However, before their meals were finished and dusk turned to night, an ear-piercing cry came from beyond their campsite.

"What was that?" The prince's uncle asked.

Although Speke heard the menacing cry while feeling a presence nearby, he was not frightened. The presence was friendly.

"It sounded like an animal, my lord," one of the soldiers replied.

After another outburst from the darkness, the prince turned to his most fearless soldier, and ordered, "Sector, I want you and two of your best men to search the perimeter." He then looked at the other soldiers, and said, "men, keep the campfires burning all night. And if you must go into the darkness to relieve yourselves, do not go alone."

Although Sector and his men had not returned from their search, the camp settled down. After consuming massive amounts of food and wine, the expedition was happy to settle quietly in their tents and rest for the night. Speke, who sat on his bed roll located in the corner of the prince's tent, contently hummed to himself while polishing his master's armor. Prince Xant and his uncle sat at a rectangular table located in the middle of their thirty-foot by twenty-foot tent. Scattered on the table were remnants of their evening meal, paper maps of the area, communication devices, and armaments.

"I don't know how you put up with that annoying humming," Toland said while nodding in Speke's direction.

Prince Xant thought about his uncle's comment and knowing that he hardly noticed Speke's humming said, "could be worse."

Toland frowned. He detested anyone that was not of noble blood. He did not understand why his nephew allowed the servant to sleep in the same tent as him. But he knew that this situation would change after they returned to their home planet: Alcean. Toland was planning a coup. His brother's illness gave him the opportunity he needed. Because his brother, the king, was ill and his nephew, the prince, was still untested; he planned that after his nephew secured the artifact, he would take it from him. He knew that whoever possessed the artifact would wield great power. And with this power, he could subjugate the other kingdoms. Moreover, through brute force, he could, once and for all, annihilate everyone with *new ways*. Although he looked at his nephew fondly, he knew that after he took the artifact from Prince Xant, he would have to kill both the prince and the king which would propel him to the head of the royal line of succession. And with the backing of his loyal soldiers, he could do just that.

"Well, my prince, I believe we should get rest. Tomorrow's a busy day," Toland said with a hint of pleasantness.

However, before Xant responded to his uncle, Sector and his two best soldiers entered the tent and patiently stood at the entrance awaiting the prince to acknowledge them.

"Approach," Xant commanded.

All three men's eyes were widened with fright and their faces were gaunt with terror. Sector approached the table, respectfully bowed his head, and reported, "my lord, we have encountered creatures like we have never seen before."

Intrigued, Xant said, "go on, explain."

"From what we could see, there were five of them. They were at least three times as tall as our spaceship."

245

"Their teeth were as tall as me!" Said one of the two soldiers that still stood at the tent's entrance.

As soon as the soldier spoke, he knew, by the look on General Toland's face, that he spoke out of turn and quickly lowered his head.

Xant thoughtfully nodded his head while considering this reconnaissance information, and asked, "what more can you tell me about these creatures?"

Losing some of his look of fright, Sector somewhat relaxed, and answered, "they stand on hind legs with a footprint as large as the tallest man. Their bodies are covered in a rugged, gravelly skin. They are impervious to our weapons. Their voices are ear-piercing closeup."

A look of fright graced Toland's face. "What do you mean that they are impervious to our weapons?"

Remembering their encounter, Sector swallowed hard. "While we were inspecting the perimeter, we were suddenly surrounded by these creatures. They came out of nowhere! I gave the order to fire on them—to light them up. We fired on them until our weapons were empty of munitions and not one of them was injured. When they began to chase us, we ran. If it were not for the campfires, they would have overtaken us."

"Logic dictates that most animals are instinctively afraid of fires; no matter how big and frightening they are. Be sure to keep the fires lit around the camp's perimeter," Prince Xant commanded.

Before either Xant or Toland asked Sector another question, a soldier entered the tent clutching the arm of a petite, slender, young woman. The brawny soldier then threw the woman to the tent's dirt floor. "My lord, I found this indigenous bitch roaming our perimeter."

246

CHAPTER 4

As the young woman attempted to stand, the soldier squarely stomped his boot into her back sending her sprawling, once again, into the dirt floor; this time face first.

"Enough!" Xant commanded. Without hesitation, he approached the woman. He then leaned down and extended his hand. Equally, without hesitation, the young woman took Xant's hand as he tenderly helped her to her feet.

After standing, the woman withdrew her hand and looked the prince directly in the eyes. Everyone in the room immediately became uncomfortable with her posture. Except for the royal family, no one looks a royal in the eyes.

While the woman defiantly stared into the leader's eyes, Xant observed her as well. Before him he saw a scantily clad, young woman. Her breasts were barely covered in a strip of burlap and her genitals were slightly covered by the same material. Her skin was mostly covered in massive, raised tattoos. These tattoos depicted images of indigenous animals, pictographs, and a foreign alphabet. Her long, dark hair appeared to have never been combed; tossed about her head in

247

matted ropes with twigs and leaves trapped between the mats.
And then there were her eyes. As Xant looked into her eyes he
felt something. Freedom? Unburdened of his destiny? He did
not know. But, seeing how the woman stared at him, he felt
small; he felt she had an amazing power behind those eyes.

Toland looked at the girl and all he felt was lust. "I will
take her to my tent and have my way with her," Toland said.
"After I am done with the savage bitch, I will pass her around
the troops for their entertainment."

Still mesmerized by the savage beauty, Xant was silent.
He did not hear what Toland said.

Afraid for the young girl, Speke rushed to the circle of
men that gathered around the girl, and said, "my lord, I believe
that the girl may be more useful than a sex toy."

Angered by Speke's outburst, Toland directed a fiery
glance at the servant, and scolded, "how dare you contradict
me!"

For the first time the girl looked directly at Speke.
Feeling her power and presence, Speke's eyes widened in
shock.

'Tell your master to examine the symbol that appears
on my upper, right arm,' the young woman *telepathically*
communicated to Speke.

Although frightened by her power to communicate
directly with his mind, Speke did as she instructed.

"My lord," Speke said, 'look at that tattoo on the
woman's upper, right arm."

Xant tore his attention from the exotic, young woman's
eyes and focused solely on her upper, right arm. Intrigued by
the marking, he moved closer to the woman. Then, without
touching her, his finger followed the drawing. "This is the
artifact which we seek," he said aloud. He then looked deeply

into her warm, brown eyes, and asked, "do you know where this object is located?"

The woman nodded.

"Will you guide me to it?" The prince asked.

With a hint of a smile, the woman slowly nodded.

Xant breathe a sigh of relief. Even though he did not know the girl, he did not want to see her passed around the soldiers like a rag doll. He looked at Speke, and said, "get the girl a bedroll and some food. She sleeps in this tent tonight."

Clearly angered by the turn of events, Toland protested, "but, nephew, this savage can surely stay in my tent. She is too dangerous to have her here with you."

Xant observed how the girl looked at his uncle. She eyed him as if he were a piece of dung underneath her feet. 'Is that how we look at our subjects?' Xant silently wondered.

"No uncle. She stays here. And she will accompany us on our expedition to the artifact site."

CHAPTER 5

That night, after the woman ate a hefty serving of venison stew, she laid down on the bed roll which was located next to Speke. With her eyes closed and laying quite still, she telepathically connected to Speke.

'So, how long have you served your master?' She asked to his mind.

Slightly alarmed by the voice in his head, Speke replied, "for about five years."

'And, he hasn't a clue about your abilities.'

'No. He doesn't know that I have *new ways.*'

'Why not?' She asked.

'He would surely kill me. People with *new ways* are a threat to the powerful people on my planet,' he answered.

'Then why do you serve him?' She asked.

'Prince Xant is a noble leader. I feel he will lead us all to live in a brighter world where we can coexist in peace. I believe that he is open to diversity.'

For a few moments, Speke was silent. Then he asked, 'does everyone on your planet have *new ways?*'

'Not everyone, but we are working on them.'
Speke thought about this and took pleasure in the
prospect of a planet with people who were mostly like him.
Then he said, 'my name is Speke, what is yours?'
'My name is Stephanie,' the girl replied.

***

The next morning, Xant led a search party of ten. The
rest of the men were ordered to stay behind and guard the
camp. Walking up front were Stephanie, Xant, Speke, and
Toland; the rest of the men trailed behind. Ahead of them was
a steep mountain approximately two-thousand feet high. This
mountain covered in tall conifer trees had an underbrush of
densely growing ferns approximately five feet tall. As they
emerged from the meadow and approached the mountain, the
ground began to shake. As the ground shook, Stephanie bolted.
With lightning speed, she ran from the edge of the meadow and
headed for a patch of ferns that was surrounded by conifers.
Instinctively, Speke and Xant followed her.

As the three hid in the underbrush, covered in ferns, the
ground violently shook. Too slow to make it to the patch of
ferns, Toland and the others were caught in the open meadow.
With dropped jaws and widened eyes, they initially froze as
they saw alien creatures approaching them. Before them were
three large carnivores. Towering over them at eight times the
height of their tallest man, these creatures, with leathery skin
and yellow eyes, displayed vicious teeth that emanated from
slobbering mouths. Besides the dangerous teeth, these vicious
creatures possessed short, stubby arms capped with razor-sharp
claws.

251

"Go back to the camp!" Xant said over his communication device to his search party.

Already running back to the camp, Toland did not respond. However, Sector—who still faced the angry animals—protested, and said "my lord, we can't leave you."

"The girl knows what she is doing," Xant said to Sector over his communication device. "I believe a smaller party will stand a better chance of finding the artifact. Go back to the camp, pack it up, wait for me at the spaceship, and I will keep you updated on our progress."

With those words, Sector and his men slowly backed away from the creatures. However, as soon as the creatures took a step towards them, they turned and broke out into a full sprint back to the camp.

Although the creatures were between him and his men, Xant saw that his men made it to the safety of their campsite. After seeing that no one was in danger, Stephanie stood from the ferns' cover, looked up at the mountain top, nodded in its direction, and began walking. With the agility of a mountain goat, she wound her way through the thick, almost impassable ferns until she came upon an animal's path. Once stepping onto the path, she glanced back at her two traveling companions who moved through the barrier-like foliage with great difficulty. Within a few moments, Xant and Speke caught up with Stephanie. Silently, Xant fell in line behind Stephanie on the narrow path and Speke brought up the rear.

Throughout his entire life, Prince Xant was never lacking in female company. For this reason, he was passivity intrigued by women. Stephanie, however, grabbed his interest. Their similarities ended with being humanoids who stood upright with a head, torso, two arms, and two legs. Stephanie's pinkish-colored skin, warm brown eyes, and black hair differed significantly from his people's violet-colored skin, pink eyes littered with flecks of gold, and green, spiked hair.

Not only was he intrigued by their outward differences, but he was also intrigued by her womanly body. While walking behind her on the narrow path, he had a close-up view of her body. The round portion of her buttocks were in clear view; the scanty loincloth barely covered her backside. Each time she moved, every muscle from her shoulders to her calves, moved with magnificent grace.

"My lord," Speke said from behind, "would you care for something to drink?"

Lost in his musing about their scout, Xant remained silent.

Not hearing an answer to his question, Speke caught up with Xant and offered him a container filled with a refreshing liquid. Seeing the container, Xant took it from Speke and caught up to Stephanie. Silently, he offered the container to her. She looked at it, and thought, 'previously, I was to be raped by all of the men in the camp. Now he offers me a refreshing drink before he takes it for himself—how curious.'

Stephanie, smiled, took a sip from the container, and handed it back to Xant. After gulping down a hefty amount, Xant handed the container back to Speke, and said, "thank you."

Never being thanked before by his prince, Speke asked, "what has come over you, my lord? You never thanked me before."

Dumbfounded why he thanked his servant, Xant mumbled, "well, I am thanking you now. There is a first time for everything."

Speke laughed, and said, "since there is a first time for everything, how about giving me a day off of work."

Prince Xant ignored that last comment.

While walking up the steep mountain-path strewn here and there with dead, fallen fir trees, wind-blown branches, and fist-sized pinecones; both Xant and Speke found themselves slipping and almost falling several times. After their third time of stumbling over a branch, Stephanie found a fallen log located adjacent to the path where she stopped walking.

"We rest here," she said.

While both men were happy for the rest, they were astounded she spoke their language.

Prince Xant and Speke sat on the two-foot in diameter log. Speke opened his satchel and laid out food and drink.

"How do you know our language?" Xant asked.

"I listen, I learn," Stephanie simply said.

Now that they could communicate, the prince had a plethora of questions.

"How many of your people live on this planet?" Xant asked.

"We have over ten-thousand here," she replied.

"Do you have weapons to defend yourselves from those creatures that attacked us?"

Stephanie shook her head.

"How do you keep them from killing you?"

"They live with us and we live with them," she answered.

While Xant and Stephanie spoke, Speke looked at his surroundings. Just like he was awestruck by the fragrant stand of trees, he wondered at the forest thick with tall pines. These pines stretched to over one-hundred feet tall. At the top and through some of the branches he saw sunlight flickering in, bringing light throughout the forest. Speke loved this lush, green world. It was nothing like his home world that was covered mostly in deserts and oceans.

"So, what you are telling me is your people and these creatures live in harmony," Xant stated.

Stephanie nodded. Then looking into Xant's large, oval pink eyes that was flecked with golden specks, she asked, "do your people live in peace?"

Xant shook his head, and answered, "no. We have many fractured kingdoms that are located throughout my world. And, my kingdom, itself, is fractured."

Although Stephanie knew about Xant's world from the briefing she received from Thia and Stash, she pretended innocence. "I don't understand," she said.

"There are individuals in our kingdoms that have abilities which the majority lack," he said. "These individuals pose a threat to the people in power."

Hearing this, Stephanie leveled Speke a glance. Knowing that Speke was secretly one of those individuals, she wanted him to enter the conversation.

"Pardon me, my lord," Speke said. "I don't consider them a threat. They have not caused violence against anyone. When all is said and done, they just wish to be left alone."

Irritated by Speke's interruption, Xant asked with a smirk, "what do you know about them?"

Speke puffed out his chest, stared Xant in the eyes, and answered, "I know things."

Noticing the challenge in Speke's voice, Xant asked, "what do *you* know?"

"I know that our leaders are afraid of these individuals because they are different from them. I know that the leaders feel that those differences will threaten their power. I know that these people have been persecuted and killed because of this perceived power struggle. And, I know that, given the chance, these people would rather be part of the citizenry than on the outside. They can make great contributions to our kingdoms."

Xant had never heard his servant speak at length about a subject. He internally agreed with almost everything Speke said. He, personally, had never felt threatened by these people with *new ways*. And, Speke was right, only the people in power perceived the threat and preached it to their kingdoms. Deep within him, Xant believed in justice—and that meant justice for all. He believed that if these outsiders followed the rules of his kingdom, then they could live peacefully there. And, although he believed in these ideals, he knew the hatred that those in power felt for these people. And, at the root of that hatred was greed.

Staring into Speke's eyes, he saw his servant anew.

"I can't believe that I am saying this, but I agree with you, Speke," Xant admitted.

Speke smiled a sigh of relief.

"However," Xant said while holding up his left hand in the manner that Speke saw him do many times when he made a decree, "it is much too complicated for one person to accomplish. It is hard to change the hearts and minds of the old guard."

"You're not just *any* person. You are a prince. And, one day you will be king. You can make the kingdom as fair and just as you wish," Speke insisted.

Before Xant answered, Stephanie—who sat on the other side of Xant—put a hand on his knee, and said, "hearts and minds on my planet were changed by a few people— *Heraclitus, Gandhi, and Dr. Martin Luther King, Jr.*—to name a few. These men, some of whom were princes, like yourself,

256

wanted justice for all people. They believed that power and light were borne out of diversity of spirit. And, through many sacrifices, little-by-little their goals came to life."

Strengthened by Stephanie's touch and inspired by her words, Xant felt the sparks of ideas growing within him. With a strength of conviction, he stood and declared, "upon securing the artifact, I will have the power to control people and make listen to me."

Seeing the doubt in Speke's face, Stephanie conveyed to him telepathically, 'it is a start.'

She also stood and continued hiking the winding path up the mountain.

CHAPTER 6

The trio continued up the steep, winding path. After traversing three switchbacks up the near vertical slope, they emerged from the forested canopy and onto a broad, treeless plateau. Even though Stephanie continued to walk, both Xant and Speke stood motionless. Astounded by their surroundings, the two, young men were awestruck. Never in their wildest imaginations could they conjure such a site. This grass and pebble covered plateau, a mile in diameter, was devoid of trees. In the place of trees, large crystals approximately ten feet tall and two feet in diameter grew out of the grass and pebble covered ground. And, although they were fascinated by the crystals that grew from the ground, what astounded them even more so were the massive crystal structures which floated overhead! These six feet in diameter, amethyst crystals were forged in individual flower arrangements which radiated out from a golden center.

Prince Xant observed the floating, purple quartz arrangements. When he realized they were not going to fall on his head and smash him, he scanned the remainder of the

258

plateau. Looking over the pebbly, grassy area, he saw at least one-hundred people seated on blankets which were strewn throughout. These people looked like Stephanie. They were listening to a band that was playing eerie music. As he perused farther, he saw the object of his hunt. For, in the center of all these people was *the artifact*. It was larger than he had imagined. The heavy, golden object, which resembled two chalices connected at their bases, stood almost six-feet tall. This polished symbol floated two feet from the pebbled ground—leaving both ends open to the environment.

"Come," Stephanie said to the two young men, "I want to introduce you to a friend of mine."

Seeing that they were still awestruck, Stephanie, standing between them, held both of their hands, and walked toward the golden altar. Before they reached the altar, Fritzie ran up to Stephanie with his arms stretched wanting to be picked up. Stephanie smiled at her little cousin, lifted him up, and rested him on her hip.

"This is Fritzie, my cousin," Stephanie said to the two men. Then in one fluid move, she handed Fritzie to Xant.

Awkwardly, Xant took the child into his arms. Before he had a chance to give him back to Stephanie, a man of considerable age approached the foursome.

"This is my friend and spiritual leader, Worm," Stephanie said.

The elder, dressed in cotton, white pants and shirt, nodded at the two young men. And even though he said nothing verbally, he connected with Speke telepathically, and said, 'we don't get many people born from *Clarity*; you are most welcome here.'

"Come," Stephanie said to the two while pointing to an empty blanket, "we sit here."

Dumbfounded by everything that has transpired, Xant did as he was told. While sitting with Fritzie on his lap, and looking at the artifact, he wondered how he could get such a heavy thing down the mountain. He thought about having his spaceship hover over the mountain top while lifting the object onboard. But, before his thoughts wandered further, he felt a tug on his shirt. Then looking down to the child that quietly sat in his lap, he was, once again, overwhelmed. He became suddenly transfixed by the child's eyes; those eyes held the wonders of the universe. Looking deeply into Fritzie's eyes, Xant's core began to fracture. His previous beliefs in his superiority quaked. Societal structures that defined his being ruptured.

Sitting on a blanket located next to Stephanie's blanket was Otto and his father, Gunther. While on their travels from Mars, they came close to, but never achieved, ten-dimensional status. Tried as they did, their minds were closed to the prospect. Although they did not achieve ten-dimensional status, they were able to glimpse the possibilities of evolving. Years of scientific and cultural thinking blocked their efforts to enlightenment.

"Nice look on you," Otto said to Stephanie referring to her transformation.

Stephanie scanned her heavily tattooed body clad in scanty burlap, shook her dreadlocks, and replied, "just having fun. Are you and your dad ready for the ceremony?"

Wanting to possess the powers that his friends had, Otto crossed his fingers, and said, "as ready as I will ever be."

Gunther, on the other hand, eyed the ceremony from an engineering point of view. He likened the golden altar to the shape of a *wormhole*, a hypothetical structure of space-time. Gunther knew this wormhole as a tunnel connecting points

260

that are separated in space and time. And, knowing all the properties of a wormhole, quartz crystal, and gold; he concluded that the entire plateau was the most sophisticated, super-conducting apparatus that he could of ever envisioned. Then as he watched Worm unwrap a crystal egg and have it float effortlessly from his arms and rest just above the golden altar's opening, he concluded that whatever was going to take place must be on a mind-altering scale! From an engineering point of view, this exquisitely mastered structure was designed to receive massive amounts of information from an energy burst that no human-made device could contain. Gunther deduced that the instant this information was received from the universe, the crystal's metaphysical properties would not only interpret the data, but also release this data so that it interacts with any living receptacle that is open to accept it. Knowing that a massive amount of information was impossible for humans to receive in their present stage, Gunther deduced that the human makeup will first have to be transformed; thus, transforming each being into a higher entity.

Everyone silenced as Worm stood before the altar with his hands raised to the sky. He now chanted to his Sioux god, Wakantanka. With his long, grey hair flowing in a strengthening wind, Worm began to glow. In response to his mesmerizing chanting and glowing body, the crystal egg that floated above the altar also glowed.

While Speke felt the wonder of the ceremony, Prince Xant's eyes were locked with the child's eyes.

Gunther witnessed the god-like Worm bathe in a bright energy field. Gunther watched as Worm's energy field expanded to all the crystals on the mountain. Upon being touched by the energy field, each crystal, whether floating above them or growing from the ground, lit up with the same intensity as the field that surrounded Worm's body. Gunther observed as the energy, which was initially confined to Worm and the crystals, now spread to everything and everyone that was on the mountain top—including him! As an engineer, Gunther never had an out-of-body experience. In the past, he closed his mind to such nonsense. Now, with the energy flowing through his body, he not only accepted this experience as truth, but he also welcomed it.

As everyone glowed with this warm bathing energy, they stop worrying about the loved ones that they left behind. They forgave everyone in their past who caused them pain and sorrow, and they opened themselves to the warm, welcoming light.

While bathe the warm light, Prince Xant sighed as he saw the beautiful woman who gave birth to him. The woman who was taken away from him early in his life: his mother. Tears filled his eyes as he felt a part of her. And, while he knew he sat on a blanket next to Stephanie, he also knew that he was now everywhere at every time. He was in his mother's arms as an infant, he was fighting a war against a neighboring kingdom, and he was soaring through the universe as a non-corporeal being. He was now part of everything and everyone.

As the sun glided beneath the horizon, and long after the altar ceased glowing, both Prince Xant and Speke found that their group of three had grown.

CHAPTER 7

Sitting on the rectangular blanket— along with Speke, Xant, and Stephanie—was Otto. New to being ten-dimensional beings, both Xant's and Otto's bodies retained the outward glows of their auras. All the answers to questions that immediately ran through Xant's mind, flowed through him. He now knew that the power he was seeking from the artifact would not help him conquer other kingdoms. He knew that this power now resided within him. His metamorphosis enabled him to see his kingdom clearly. He saw both the limits of his kingdom's present and endless possibilities of its future.

Even though he had the answers to all these questions. One question remained unanswered. Astutely seeing Speke for the first time, he realized that Speke was much more than a servant. With renewed vision, Prince Xant saw a strong, powerful aura that emanated from this man.

"Why?" Xant asked Speke. "Why did you hide your true self from me?"

In his usual joking tone, Speke said, "if I told you who I truly were, you would have chopped my head off."

263

'I probably would have,' Xant thought.

'That's why I kept silent,' Speke telepathically communicated to Xant.

Xant's eyes widened, and he said aloud, "were you just in my head?"

Realizing the power that his servant always possessed, Xant said aloud, "by the strength of your aura, I see that you are a powerful being. Why have you reduced yourself to servitude?"

"I serve you, my prince, because I believe that you are fair and just," Speke said aloud. "And I believe that when you become king, that you will rule with fairness and bring everyone together; even those with *new ways*. I also believe that my service to you will aid in this transformation of our kingdom; maybe transforming all kingdoms on our planet."

Xant found himself nodding in agreement with Speke, and admitted, "you are more of a man than I am. Together we can bring your vision of our world into reality."

Otto, who silently sat on the blanket, now spoke up. "Hello Speke, my name is Otto. I have so many questions for you. This ceremony helped me evolve to a ten-dimensional being. Before, no matter how hard I tried, my mind was not open to such possibilities. Now that I am such an entity, I see that you are truly different from us: those who chose to evolve."

Speke nodded, and said, "I was born this way. I was born from *Clarity*."

With those words, everyone became silent.

Then breaking the silence, Otto asked, "would you join me over there." He pointed to an empty blanket, "I have so many questions that I know you could answer."

Speke smiled, stood up, and walked away with Otto.

Left alone on their blanket, Prince Xant and Stephanie laid on their backs and looked up at the darkening sky. They watched as one-by-one stars began to burst into view. "You are lucky to live on such a beautiful world with enlightened people," Xant said as he kept his eyes on the stars. "How many of your kind live here?"

Telepathically, Stephanie communicated to Xant, and answered, 'a little over ten-thousand.'

Feeling a sadness in the young woman's thoughts, Xant unknowingly communicated telepathically back to Stephanie, and said, 'tell me about your people.'

This time, Stephanie not only communicated telepathically with words to Xant, but also with pictures.

'My people are not originally from this planet. We are not even from this galaxy. My galaxy is almost thirty-million light-years from here. And my planet was called: Earth.'

Xant smiled as he saw the images of Stephanie's planet. A lush, green planet with vast, deep oceans of water. This lush planet contained—among many other things—a plethora of trees, a diversity of life, and a multitude of technically developed societies.

'How many people lived on your planet?' He asked.

'Almost eight-billion people," Stephanie replied.

Feeling Stephanie's sorrow, Xant asked, 'if there is only ten-thousand people living here on Zenti, are the rest of them still living on your planet, Earth?'

Stephanie's pain flowed to Xant as she mentally whispered, 'the rest of them are dead. They are all dead.'

Although Xant felt her pain and at the same time saw tears roll down the beautiful, young woman's face, he had to know what happened. So, he asked, 'how could eight-billion people die?'

Even though reliving the devastation her planet endured saddened Stephanie, she knew that if Xant took the plight of her planet to heart, his planet will be a force for *Clarity* and would brighten the universal light. 'Eight-billion people died because of greed,' she answered. 'Throughout thousands of years of human history, while humans survived countless wars and pandemics, greed was always there. This greed lived in a small group of people who retained their power throughout the ages by oppressing the masses. My community of two thousand was persecuted by these people. We created the technology that allowed us to escape Earth and travel to this galaxy. And, while we escaped Earth, conflict between its nations escalated. Finally, these greedy, powerful people were responsible for the most horrific war in Earth's history. They unleashed a nuclear war where country after country fought their enemies with powerful, unimaginable weapons. These weapons were so powerful that the planet's human population was significantly reduced. Moreover, the bombardments from these powerful weapons pushed the Earth out of its orbit which disrupted the Earth-Moon balance. Fortunately, our spiritual leader, Worm, knew about this and alerted us.'

Stephanie flooded Xant's mind with images of the Moon crashing into Earth while simultaneously, seeing a small subset of Earthlings escaping in massive spaceships.

'We were able to rescue thousands,' Stephanie continued. 'And, recently, Worm alerted us to a Martian colony of about two-thousand Earthlings who were doomed because of massive volcanic eruptions.' She now pushed those images to Xant's mind.

While staring at the stars, Xant instantly realized that the same fate awaited his planet if he did nothing to prevent its doom.

As the night began to darken and the starlit, moonless sky took shape, Stephanie glanced over to the prince who lay next to her. Since his deep-violet skin color blended into the darkness, Stephanie saw only two large, egg-shaped pink eyes that sparkled with golden flecks. While she silently reminisced about the past—about so many innocent souls dying because of greed—she simultaneously rejoiced for the present and the future. Although still a young adult, Stephanie had the wisdom that is only attributed to wise elders. Even though it was painful to momentarily live in the past, she reveled in the present and rejoiced in the future.

Prince Xant and Stephanie shared each other's thoughts until dawn. Not only did she give him an insight into his planet's future, but she showed him ways to use his new abilities.

As the sun peeped above the horizon, Otto, Speke, Zeke, Pulo, Fly, Gregory, Alicia, Heather, and Fritzie surrounded Stephanie's and Xant's blanket.

Xant looked up at the young people who surrounded his blanket with squinting eyes, and said, "I suppose that it is time that Speke and I return to our planet."

Stephanie nodded.

After the two of them stood to join the circle of friends, Stephanie introduced the rest of them to Xant.

Otto, who still glowed with a vibrant aura, said aloud, "now that I am a ten-dimensional being, I will join in the send-off party!"

CHAPTER 8

Prince Xant and Speke stood surrounded by ten, new friends. Without a word, they all simultaneously disappeared from the mountain and instantaneous reappeared a quarter of a mile from the prince's spaceship.

Smiles graced both Xant's and Speke's faces as they watched all, but Stephanie, transform themselves into towering, vicious-looking dinosaurs. And, as the group transformed, Stephanie also transformed. Her dreadlocks were gone; her hair was, once again, silky black. The raised tattoos were gone; her skin was pink and smooth. And her body was no longer scantly clothed in burlap; she wore a cotton, blue, knee-length dress.

While looking at Stephanie, Xant said, "I suppose, this is your true look. I like it."

Stephanie winked at him and nodded.

"So," Xant said aloud while looking up at the creatures that surrounded them, "it was your friends that frightened my people."

"Stephanie grinned, and said, "as you now know—now that you are a ten-dimensional being and you can interact with every rock, tree, and creature on a molecular level—we cannot have other non-enlightened people come to our world. If others come to our world and trample the ground, cut trees, kill animals; they are also trampling on us, dismembering us, and killing us."

Speke nodded and added, "so you make your planet as hostile looking as possible."

Stephanie added, "we also make it hard to find. The only reason you found it is because we guided you here. And we expect that you and your people will tell tales of a hostile planet."

"That's the story, and I am sticking to it," Prince Xant promised.

Stephanie hugged the prince, then said, "if you need any help with your planet, just call on us. We are but a whisper away."

Before the prince said another word, both he and Speke watched as Stephanie transformed into a massive, vicious-looking monster that was much taller than their spaceship. Then the two men heard a gentle voice in their minds, that said, 'run.'

Keeping the pretense, the prince and Speke ran at a full sprint back to their ship followed closely by ten, blood-thirsty creatures.

CHAPTER 9

When Toland saw the prince and Speke rush toward the ship followed by massive, hungry creatures with drooling, opened mouths, they immediately opened the high-bay doors.

"After we are inside, close the doors immediately and prepare to take off!" The prince commanded over his communication device.

Once the prince and Speke were onboard, they went to their stations. The prince seated himself in the primary, command chair next to his uncle.

As the spaceship lifted off, Toland was grateful to get away from the inhospitable planet. Sitting next to the prince, he asked, "did you secure the artifact?"

Prince Xant looked at his uncle and truly saw him for the first time. He knew his uncle's plans. He knew that upon securing the artifact that his uncle planned to kill both him and his father, take the artifact, and eventually conquer the entire planet.

"There was no artifact, uncle," the prince said. "It was all rumors and myths."

270

His uncle's face sank.

"Sector!" Xant commanded.

Upon the utterance of his name, Prince Xant's top general immediately snapped to the prince's side, and asked, "my lord?"

"Arrest my uncle. Remove my uncle to the brig and keep him under watch until we return to our home world," the prince commanded.

Once Sector took the stunned member of the royal family away, Xant winked at Speke who stood working at the spaceship's controls, and telepathically said, 'my friend, we have our work cut out for us.'

'You have my allegiance, my lord,' Speke communicated back.

CHAPTER 10

The ten friends—exhausted after chasing the prince and his servant—changed back into humans. Although exhausted, they laughed heartily.

"This is almost as fun as the *lacrosse* game you taught me," Pulo said to Zeke.

"*Lacrosse!*" Gregory exclaimed. "I always wanted to learn that game."

"You will. I will teach you," Zeke said. "But not today. Stash and Thia have another assignment for us. We are to meet them in the conference room."

"The quest for *Clarity* never rests," Stephanie said sweetly.

THE END

About the Author

C.E. Bradley is an accomplished scientist of 30 years who has also enjoyed both reading and writing *soft* science fiction. Author of previously published: *The Evangeline Forecast, The Herd in the Highest, The Hellenes Oracle—Prophesy 544, Virgo G.C. and Zentians; C.E.* Bradley tells stories that combine science, society, and futuristic thinking. C.E. Bradley lives in the mountains of Oregon where she continues to write.

Other Reads

By

C.E. Bradley

The Evangeline Forecasts

Experience both physical and metaphysical realms of possibilities through this breathtakingly adventurous science-fiction collection of short stories. Follow two cadets as they brave the **Black Expanse**; witness a poor boy's rise to greatness as he rescues both humanity and the entire universe from certain doom in **Brilliance**; observe a woman's awakening to the possibility of alien visitations in **The Court of two Sisters**; and many more…

The Herd in the Highest

The Herd in the Highest is the first novel in the **Home World Saga** series that chronicles two souls as they evolve over time. Through time and space, these two souls, Stash and Jenny meet, fall in love, and eventually become a couple.

274

During their journeys, Stash and Jenny encounter life-threating events inflicted on them by alien beings who intend to keep them apart. Traveling to vast regions of the Earth while surrounded by magnificent scenery, Stash and Jenny meet a variety of cultures whose spiritualities help them escape these aliens; and, subsequently, leave Earth.

Hellenes' Oracle—Prophesy 544

Hellenes' Oracle—Prophesy 544 is the second novel in the **Home World Saga** series about the journey of a group of approximately two-thousand Earthlings who departed Earth in search of a new home. Leading this group are the two, main characters, Stash and Jenny, who must face complete moral, metaphysical, and ethical transformations to obtain the location of their destination.

Exploring the edge where science meets both religion and mythology is a prevailing, underlying theme. This theme is carried out through the interactions of Greek, mythological characters based in an alternate reality.

Virgo G.C.

Besieged throughout human history by several alien beings (gods), of different stages of evolution, who manipulated

275

Earth's human development through both altering human's DNA and handing down oppressive, moral codes; two, old souls, Thia (Jenny) and Stash, escape the planet, Earth, on a quest to a far-off galaxy with a mission to destroy the oldest god of all and usher in a new era of enlightenment for all humanity.

Journey with Stash and Thia as they lead a community of two thousand through unimaginable parts of deep Space while encountering a variety of both hostile and friendly alien beings. Ride with them in a sophisticated spaceship, which takes its designs from the latest Quantum Physics theories.

This is the third book in the *Home World Saga* series.

Zentians

What if unscrupulous, presidential politics resulted in the complete obliteration of planet Earth?

In six days, everything on the planet, Earth, will change forever. Follow the lives of two, young lovers: Eva and Julian, as they struggle to survive a post-apocalyptic Earth. Escape with Eva, Julian and over eight-thousand, fellow Earthlings as they witness the complete destruction of their beloved planet. Ride with these refugees in a technologically advanced spaceship as they leave the Milky Way Galaxy, travel to the

Virgo Galactic Cluster, and subsequently, the Sombrero Galaxy where they settle on the planet, Zenti. Evolve with the refugee community as they battle to defend the entire universe from powerful, interdimensional beings.

Zentians is the fourth novel in the ***Home World Saga*** series.

Made in the USA
Monee, IL
15 December 2022

21631115R00154